"I suggest we approach marriage first and address the reasons later."

"What are the reasons?" Princess Megan dared challenge Jean-Paul with her gaze when he cast her a direct stare.

Finally he shrugged. "The child, assuming there is one…"

She folded her hands in her lap to conceal her trembling.

"There's the passion," he continued. His lips curved ever so slightly into a smile that mocked them both. "I want to make love to you each time I see you. I think you feel the same."

"It's only lust.… I will not marry for your convenience, nor for the sake of protocol."

"Stop being childish and accept the fate that has been preordained for us," Jean-Paul ordered.

Before he realized what she was doing, she leapt out of his arms and was gone.…

Dear Reader,

April may bring showers, but it also brings in a fabulous new batch of books from Silhouette Special Edition! This month treat yourself to the beginning of a brand-new exciting royal continuity, CROWN AND GLORY. We get the regal ball rolling with Laurie Paige's delightful tale *The Princess Is Pregnant!* This romance is fair to bursting with passion and other temptations.

I'm pleased to offer *The Groom's Stand-In* by Gina Wilkins— a fascinating story that is sure to keep readers on the edge of their seats…and warm their hearts in the process. Peggy Webb is no stranger herself to heartwarming romance with the next installment of her miniseries THE WESTMORELAND DIARIES. In *Force of Nature,* a beautiful photojournalist encounters a primitive man in the wilderness and must find a way to tame his oh-so-wild heart.

In *The Man in Charge*, Judith Lyons gives us a tender reunion romance where an endangered chancellor's daughter finds herself being guarded by the man she's never been able to forget—a rugged mercenary who's about to learn he's the father of their child! And in Wendy Warren's new sensation *Dakota Bride,* readers will relish the theme of learning to love again, as a young widow dreams of love and marriage with a handsome stranger. In addition, you'll find an intriguing case of mistaken identity in Jane Toombs's *Trouble in Tourmaline*, where a world-weary lawyer takes a breather from his fast-paced life and finds his sights brightened by a lovely psychologist, who takes him for a gardener. You won't want to put this story down!

So kick back and enjoy the fantasy of falling in love, and be sure to return next month for another winning selection of emotionally satisfying and uplifting stories of love, life and family!

Best,

Karen Taylor Richman
Senior Editor

Please address questions and book requests to:
Silhouette Reader Service
U.S.: 3010 Walden Ave., P.O. Box 1325, Buffalo, NY 14269
Canadian: P.O. Box 609, Fort Erie, Ont. L2A 5X3

The Princess Is Pregnant!

LAURIE PAIGE

Silhouette®

SPECIAL EDITION™

Published by Silhouette Books

America's Publisher of Contemporary Romance

Special thanks and acknowledgment
are given to Laurie Paige for her contribution
to the CROWN AND GLORY series.

To the new moms: Nancy and Wendy
and the new babies: Josephine and Logan.

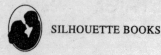 SILHOUETTE BOOKS

ISBN 0-373-24459-2

THE PRINCESS IS PREGNANT!

Visit Silhouette at www.eHarlequin.com

Printed in U.S.A.

Books by Laurie Paige

LAURIE PAIGE

says, "In the interest of authenticity, most writers will try anything...once." Along with her writing adventures, Laurie has been a NASA engineer, a past president of the Romance Writers of America, a mother and a grandmother. She was twice a Romance Writers of America RITA® Award finalist for Best Traditional Romance, and has won awards from *Romantic Times* for Best Silhouette Special Edition and Best Silhouette. Recently resettled in Northern California, Laurie is looking forward to whatever experiences her next novel will send her on.

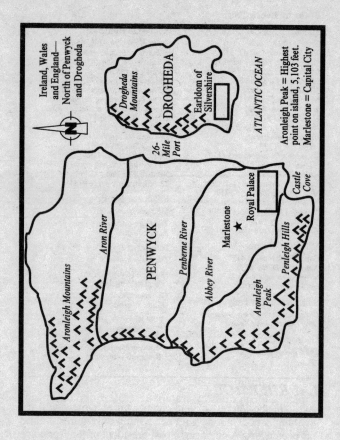

Ireland, Wales and England— North of Penwyck and Drogheda

N

Drogheda Mountains

DROGHEDA

Earldom of Silvershire

ATLANTIC OCEAN

Aronleigh Peak = Highest point on island, 5,103 feet.
Marlestone = Capital City

26-Mile Port

Aronleigh Mountains

Aron River

PENWYCK

Penberne River

Abbey River

Marlestone

★

Royal Palace

Aronleigh Peak

Penleigh Hills

Castle Cove

Chapter One

The princess is pregnant! The princess is pregnant!

Princess Megan Penelope Penwyck felt everyone in the palace was thinking those very words as she walked up the polished marble steps and crossed the reception chamber where guards, maids, diplomats and dignitaries watched, dusted or conferred in small clusters, each intent on his or her own task and paying absolutely no heed to anyone else.

Except she knew the latter wasn't true.

Everything that went on in the island kingdom of Penwyck, located in the Atlantic Ocean off the coast of Britain, was noted and commented upon by the denizens of the country, by the press and by heads of state of other countries.

She recalled a saying appropriate to the moment: *These are the times that try men's souls.* Women's souls were vulnerable, too. In her own mind, she'd been tried, convicted and sentenced to the firing squad.

Don't be melodramatic, she chided her quivering spirits. When the news did get out, as it invariably must, everyone in the kingdom would be shocked that Megan, the quiet princess, the introspective one, was expecting a child…out of wedlock.

A wry, uncertain smile curved her lips as Megan approached the door to the king's official chambers.

Her father, King Morgan, had been pleased with her written report on the world trade conference. Her appointment with him was to discuss the results of the talks and decide the tiny island kingdom's next course of action.

She tried to ignore the tremor that ran through every nerve in her body as she recalled the conference held in Monaco eight weeks ago. The second week of April, to be exact. It was now Monday of the second week in June.

And she was two months pregnant. Two pregnancy tests, bought and used in great secrecy on her part, had confirmed the shocking news.

She'd had no word from Jean-Paul Augustuve—Earl of Silvershire, heir to a dukedom in the neighboring island country of Drogheda and father of her child—in answer to the note she'd dispatched to him two weeks ago.

Another tremor rushed through her as she paused outside the door leading to the king's busy public quarters. The doorman smiled and bowed her into the Royal Secretary's office. The room was empty.

"Your Royal Highness," a familiar voice greeted her.

Sir Selywyn Estabon, the royal secretary, entered from the king's audience chamber and bowed graciously, his dark eyes mesmerizing, his skin pale from long hours spent inside each day. At thirty-five, six feet tall and muscular looking, Selywyn was a handsome, intriguing man, seemingly devoted to his job.

As teenagers, she and her sisters had spun endless daydreams about him and had speculated on his eligibility as a royal spouse. He'd paid absolutely no heed to their girlish flirting, thus their fantasies had withered and died a natural death as the three girls matured.

Selywyn was intensely loyal to their father and protective of the royal family. Megan knew him to be totally trustworthy with secrets of state or of the heart. All the royal offspring had confided in him over the years.

She swallowed with difficulty. She'd shared her latest secret with no one yet. "Good morning, Sir Selywyn," she responded. "I have an appointment, I believe?" she added when the secretary made no move to usher her into the king's presence. Her father wasn't one to be kept waiting.

"The king sends his regrets, but he will be unable to meet with you this morning."

Selywyn could have no idea how relieved Megan felt. She nearly flung herself into his arms and showered him with kisses of gratitude. The imaginary firing squad lowered their guns and she was able to breathe deeply once more.

"I'm sorry for the inconvenience," the man added.

She managed a nod. "Shall I reschedule?"

In the pause that followed, she detected uncertainty in his eyes, then it was gone. Apprehensive again, she studied the king's secretary, knowing that he was privy to all that went on in the kingdom, and expected bad news, but nothing more was forthcoming.

"I will call you if the king has further questions." The secretary smiled slightly. "Your report was very comprehensive. King Morgan was pleased."

At twenty-seven, Megan had long ago learned to contain her emotions, but she felt a tiny glow at the secondhand praise. The royal siblings had always vied for their father's limited time, and it was a special reward to receive recognition for one's work on behalf of the kingdom.

"Please convey my thanks," she said modestly, and left the office as Selywyn held the door. She was clearly but kindly dismissed.

Which was fine by her. The king would not be

pleased at her personal news. Unless it aided the affairs of state, she added, frowning. She would *not* be used as a treaty between two nations the way royal family members had been used in days of old. Even her parents' marriage had been arranged.

Thinking of the coming months, she trembled like a leaf caught in a gale while worry laced through her composure.

Instead of using the public entry-exit as one was supposed to when seeking or leaving a royal audience, she quickly escaped the huge reception chamber through a side door. A dash through the formal gardens, open to all, and through a gate with a coded lock brought her to the palace's private gardens where the royals—the three girls and the twins, Owen and Dylan—had played under the watchful eyes of nannies and guards and their mother, Queen Marissa.

For a moment, Megan sat on a stone bench and inhaled the scent of June roses washed clean by the early morning fog. The worry subsided in the tranquillity of the garden.

Finally, drawn irresistibly by the sea, she rose, slipped through another locked gate and walked along the shore path. The trail dropped from a height of forty feet at the knoll, where the original palace had been built nearly four hundred years ago, to the shore in gently rolling swells as if the ocean had etched its restless nature on the land aeons ago. Here, a secluded cove embraced a beach of sand and shells and scattered rocks. Farther out, huge boulders formed a curving breakwater shielding a tiny island in the middle of the bay.

Megan stood on the shore and watched the waves rush in ripples from the Atlantic to break on the shores of Penwyck and its neighbors, Drogheda and Majorco. To the east lay England, Ireland and Wales. Fed by currents that arose in the Caribbean, the ocean brought both cooling breezes and the warmth of the equator to temper their climate. In some sheltered coves, palm trees grew.

Pressing her hands against her heart, she tried to still the great restless longing that rose there. She'd held her worries at bay by dint of will, but her defenses crumbled all at once like a cliff face that could bear the pounding of the waves no longer.

She remembered another night, another sea...

The evening reception was dull. Elegantly dressed dignitaries and their wives, or husbands, as the case may be, moved about the ballroom of the hotel in an ever-changing kaleidoscope of faces, the topics of conversation as varied as the countries represented at the International Trade Conference in Monte Carlo. She was there representing Penwyck in lieu of her older sister—Meredith, the Intelligent One, as the eldest Penwyck princess was known affectionately by their countrymen—who'd been called to other, more urgent, duties at the last minute.

Megan was bored, tired after a week of endless speeches and diatribes, not to mention lunches, dinners and cocktail parties every night. She really preferred her own silent company to all this noise.

Grimacing at how terribly vain that sounded, she glanced around as if looking for an escape route.

At the back corner of the room, she spied a tall masculine figure slipping into the shadows of the terrace. Another soul who needed to escape. She knew who he was.

On impulse, she followed.

Bolted was more like it, she admitted with a carefree laugh as she ducked through the door, which was slightly ajar, and into the star-glazed Mediterranean night. The casinos of Monte Carlo were brightly lit and doing a bustling business. The moon was huge. Its light silvered everything in its glow.

She spotted the lithe frame of Jean-Paul Augustuve as he strolled purposefully toward the marina. She knew he kept a sailboat there, an oceangoing ketch that he could sail alone. She'd never been invited on it, although she'd seen photos of other royal offspring or world-famous models smiling from its teak decks in newspapers from time to time.

Beautiful, competent women who knew their place in the world. Or forged one for themselves.

Megan hesitated, for those traits didn't describe her at all, then hurried to keep up with his long strides. They arrived at the boat slip, with her not more than ten feet behind him.

"What do you want?" he asked, swinging around to face her after he stepped aboard.

She started in surprise, sure he hadn't known she was near. "I wondered if you were going for a sail."

Hearing the uncertainty in her voice, she groaned internally. He would never mistake her for one of those confident women he favored.

His eyes, dark now but a brilliant blue in daylight, studied her for a long, nerve-racking moment, then his teeth flashed in a smile. "Yes."

She gripped the material at each side of her silk gown. "I want to go with you."

"No."

The refusal didn't surprise her—she'd never expected him to notice her—but it did hurt a bit. The hot press of tears stung her eyes. She was suddenly angry, with herself for the weakness of weeping and with him for his cruel indifference to her feelings.

"Why?" she demanded, surprising both of them.

"I want to be alone."

"So do I."

"Then find your own boat."

"I won't get in your way," she promised. "I know how to sail. You might need my help."

Again the white flash that appeared almost ghostly in the silvery light. He unfastened one of the mooring lines.

"She's a true lady," he said of his ship. "She responds to only one hand—mine."

The sure arrogance along with a second rebuff dissolved the unusual anger. The odd pain flowed over her again.

Megan thought of cold things, of icy fjords and glaciers, of herself as the Ice Princess, remote, cold, untouchable. It was a device she'd used since she was a child—to simply remove her emotions from the situation and lock them in ice. It worked this time, too.

She took one step back on the dock, away from the sailboat and the handsome, arrogant Earl of Silvershire and his wish to be alone.

He moved about the deck effortlessly, fluidly, seemingly one with the night, a fairy prince spawned of something as insubstantial as sea foam and moondust. Nourished by sea and moonlight, he needed nothing from one as mortal as she. Lifting her chin, she turned away.

"Cast off the other line," he ordered softly and stepped toward the tiller.

Surprised, she spun and caught a flash of silver from his eyes as he glanced her way. She slipped the line from the mooring, took two running steps as the ship swung away from the dock and leaped to the deck.

The action would have been a small step for Jean-Paul Augustuve; it was a giant leap for Megan

Penelope Penwyck. Would she land in a safe harbor? Or in a foreign port amidst the gravest danger?

An engine throbbed to life and the ship eased from the slip and into the black-and-pewter waters of the sea. Once away from the marina and the crowded shoreline, Jean-Paul cut the engine and hoisted the sail. They sailed silently on the silver path where the moon met the sea.

"Out here like this," he said in a voice that murmured over her like the sound of the sea and the night wind, "I sometimes imagine that I'll sail right off the end of the earth."

"What will you find?" she asked, intensely curious about his fantasy.

"Never-never land, perhaps. I always wanted to be Peter Pan and sail the heavens on great adventures."

His soft laughter, aimed at himself and a boy's foolish dreams, broke through the ice dam and touched her heart.

Jean-Paul was known as something of a rebel and one of the world's most sought after bachelors, but here was another side to him that was usually hidden, one that was whimsical and tender with dreams that could never be realized.

She'd sometimes felt like that.

A bond, she realized, and wondered if he felt it, too, and if that had prompted his confidence. His next words dispelled that notion.

"Sit down before you fall overboard," he ordered, his tone sardonic, as if it wouldn't bother him at all if that should happen.

She ducked as the wind grabbed the sail and the boom shifted. Jean-Paul swung them around so that they ran with the wind. He motioned for her to sit on the bench with him.

The wind snatched her hair from the circle of flowers that secured it to the back of her head, and blew tendrils around her face. Her breath nearly stopped when he reached over to her and began pulling the long pins loose and tossing them over the side.

When she glanced at him, no smile lit his lean face. Instead he appeared thoughtful, almost angry as he frowned at some conflict that showed briefly in his eyes then was hidden from her.

Confused, she watched as he lifted the circlet of flowers, studied it for a long moment, then brought it to his lips the way a lover might who mourned his lost love and tossed it into the night.

Her heart clenched so tightly she thought it would explode from the pressure as she watched the wreath land in the dark water, catch a moonbeam and float out of sight. She pushed the hair from her eyes and held it back with hands that trembled ever so slightly.

With another glance she didn't understand, Jean-Paul turned the ship once more and sailed on a tack into the wind. Tendrils of hair blew back from her temples.

"Let it go," he commanded.

She slowly dropped her hands to her lap. He lifted one hand and slid his fingers into the tangles.

"Like silk," he said in a low tone that stirred turmoil within her.

When his hand dropped to her bare shoulder, she started, then retreated behind the icy facade.

"I've wanted to do this all evening," he continued, and stroked across her back, along the edge of the silk, until his arm was around her. His fingers caressed slowly up and down her arm, causing chills, which he then smoothed away.

Disappointment swamped her when he withdrew his arm and set the vessel on a different tack across the wind. She watched the shoreline as they raced parallel to it. At last he spilled the wind from the sail and engaged the engine again to push into a small cove similar to the one at Penwyck where she'd learned to swim and sail years ago.

"You seem to know these waters well," she said.

"Yes."

Sudden, intense jealousy flamed in her, then died as she further retreated from emotion. She was nothing to him; he was nothing to her. There was no need for this reaction.

"I love the sea," she said to distract herself from his allure. "At home, we have a private place, a cove behind the palace where we played and learned to swim. The bay there is small, but it was a world to us, a place of freedom..."

She let the thought trail off, aware that she gave too much of herself away to this worldly man. What did he care about her need for freedom, to secret herself away from the rest of civilization and live her own fantasy?

He watched her, a slight puzzlement in his eyes. "Who are you?" he asked in a quiet tone.

A current ran along her nerves at the question that was as whimsical as his desire to sail off into the moonlight. The bond grew stronger...more urgent.

"Megan," she finally answered, a hitch in her breath as possibilities opened to her. She wanted... she wanted...oh, stars and moonlight and rapture.

Foolish, foolish Megan, the Ice Princess scolded.

"Not your name," he corrected. "The real you. Ah, yes, the Quiet One."

She tensed at the nickname, but he said nothing more, only watched her from eyes hooded by thick lashes, the lean planes of his face harsh and forbidding. She shivered.

He stood, then quickly threw out the anchor and furled the sail. He went into the hold. In another minute, soft music swelled into the darkness. He returned and held out his arms in invitation to dance.

The first time they'd danced had been at Meredith's birthday ball. Jean-Paul had politely danced with all the royals, starting with the birthday girl, then the queen and finally her. Anastasia had attended the dinner, then been sent to bed, but Megan had been allowed to stay. Those moments in his arms had seemed filled with magic.

This evening was to be a seduction, she realized. That was what he had decided she wanted. He, with his vast knowledge of many women, knew nothing of her. Looking at the challenge in his eyes, she was tempted, so very tempted.

But this night wasn't for her. She shook her head.

"No?" he mocked.

"I want to be alone," she said, turning his earlier statement on him and allowing no emotion to show on her face. Rising, she made her way to the bow and stood watching the luminous rush of shallow waves to the beach.

Disappointment raged through her, although she wasn't shocked. She didn't know what she'd expected from her impulsive action, but it hadn't been this blatant invitation to pleasure, given without words or tender feelings, an intimate meeting of strangers, as it were.

The engine throbbed to life under her feet. Slowly he turned the ketch until they were safely away from the rocky shore. He was returning her to the marina.

She wasn't surprised, she wasn't even hurt, but she did regret her rashness in following him.

With the sail up, they tacked against the wind

once more, sailing westward rather than eastward toward the port.

Turning, she studied him at the helm, his touch sure and experienced as he guided them out to sea. She wondered if he headed for Gibraltar and the vast ocean beyond. They would sail to the new world…or perhaps all the way home. His or hers?

The island principality of Drogheda was twenty-six miles from her father's kingdom of Penwyck. Jean-Paul's uncle was the ruling prince, his father a powerful duke. Jean-Paul, as heir apparent, had been named Earl of Silvershire at twenty-one, much as the future king of England was vested as Prince of Wales when he came of age.

An earl was a suitable husband for a royal princess.

The idea shocked and excited and saddened her. If they married, it would be an official marriage, a merger between two ancient enemies who had tried to conquer each other since the time of Arthur Pendragon and his knights.

She faced the wind and let it blow the silvery webs of longing from her heart. She would never marry. It wasn't in the cards.

"The sea is getting rough," Jean-Paul called to her. "Come astern now. Grab a life preserver from the locker."

She reluctantly did as told and rejoined him at the helm. He had removed his tuxedo jacket, shoes and socks, she saw. His shirt was open to the waist. He'd rolled the cuffs up and out of his way.

He motioned for her to sit, then dropped a rain slicker over her head and arranged its folds to cover her evening gown. His glance at her feet reminded her of the silver sandals she wore. She kicked them off and tossed them down the hatch into the hold.

He grinned and secured the hatch against the squall that was coming up. "I know a place," he said, as if to reassure her he knew what he was doing.

She nodded.

Just as rain and the first rough wave broke over the bow, he turned the sailing yacht toward a long sea wall, scooted around its end and into a protected cove.

In the sudden stillness, Megan felt her heart pound. Her mouth went dry. They would most likely have to spend the remainder of the night here. She couldn't decide how she felt about that.

Did she want to be seduced? Was the unconscious wish for fulfillment the driving force behind this strange adventure? Ever honest, she tried to answer, but soon gave it up as hopeless.

After he secured the ship, he opened the hatch and gestured for her to precede him. She went down the steps and stopped. He lifted the poncho over her head and hung it on a hook, then did the same with his shirt. From a cabinet, he removed two towels and tossed one to her. When he dried his hair, she did the same to hers.

The narrow space of the galley was much too restrictive for two people. His elbow bumped hers. His hip touched hers when he tossed the towel on the hook over his shirt, then moved past her to the galley stove.

"Coffee?" he asked, already starting the preparation.

She nodded, then said yes. "Please," she added.

He paused in measuring water into the pot and stared at her for a breath-catching ten seconds. His smile warmed her as he bent to his task once more. "I love to hear a woman beg," he murmured with wicked amusement.

"Don't," she requested. "I don't play games."

He set the pot to brewing, then leaned a hip against the counter and perused her. She smoothed her hair as much as possible.

"Sometimes I don't, either. Turn around," he said, and took a brush from a drawer.

He turned her with hands on her shoulders, then proceeded to brush the tangles until her hair hung smooth around her shoulders. He brushed his own dark locks in a few impatient strokes and tossed the brush back into the drawer.

"Beautiful," he said as if he spoke to himself.

He ran his hand down her hair from the crown of her head to the ends, then he let his hand glide down her back. Goose bumps sprang into being all along her arms. When he guided her so that she faced him once more, she let him.

Their eyes met and held, his intensely blue, confident, arrogant even, hers green and unsure because that was the way she felt. Her heart questioned what was happening, but she shied from the answer. She really didn't know.

He gave his head a little shake, and she realized the questions were in him, too. Neither of them quite knew why they were together, why they were alone on a ship in a storm, why the night seemed different.

Slowly she became aware of his heat. His chest was only inches from hers. His thumbs caressed the hollows of her shoulders with gentle strokes that were fiery and wonderful at the same time.

Inhaling was an effort. So was lifting her hands and laying them on his chest. Muscles tensed under her fingers as she moved them restlessly over his hard flesh.

He wasn't a brawny man, but his masculine strength was evident in the lithe definition of his torso, the ropy musculature of his shoulders and arms. He was a man who worked and played hard.

And for keeps?

She tossed her head at the foolish question. She wasn't expecting forever. So what, exactly, was she asking for?

"What?" he questioned, his eyes narrowing as if he witnessed the confusion inside her.

"Nothing."

"I'm going to kiss you," he warned a second before he did. His lips were intensely warm on hers.

She opened her mouth, but no protest came out. He took the kiss deeper, his tongue sweeping over her lips in long moments of sweet sampling before seeking more.

Fire erupted within her. Weakened by the heat, she leaned into him, experiencing him fully as their chests, bellies and thighs pressed hotly into one flesh.

Her breasts beaded and swelled, pushing against the confines of the support built into the silk.

His hands shifted so that his thumbs caressed just above the material. Then, so suddenly she couldn't have anticipated it, he dipped one hand inside and lifted her breast into his palm, its tip wantonly seeking his touch.

When he lifted his head, he muttered something not quite audible, but she didn't need the words. She knew in her soul what they were. She, too, felt the wonder.

They kissed again, more urgently this time. He stepped forward, his thigh making a space between hers so that their caresses became more enticing. She found herself reacting instinctively, knowing without words or past experience all that she needed to do.

After exploring the length of his back, she stretched up on tiptoe and ran her hands over his powerful shoulders, then up his neck and into his hair. He wore it somewhat longer than the current style. She gathered a handful and held on while their kiss rocketed through her again.

At last he caught her hands in both of his and held them behind her back, bending her slightly so he could reach the tingling flesh of her breasts above her gown.

Then he slid one hand to the zipper. And stopped.

When she opened her eyes, he said, "No games, right?"

She nodded.

"Come with me."

It was a request. She laid her hand in his. They went to the stern, where a bed filled almost all the available space. The bed wasn't prepared for instant seduction, she saw and was glad.

She helped him spread sheets and tuck them in. The air had grown chill, so he added a comforter. Then he turned to her, placed his hands on the fastening at his waistband and waited for her consent.

In that instant she knew she could never say he gave her no choice. The decision was hers. She turned her back to him and lifted her hair out of the way.

He slid the zipper of her dress down, then helped her step out of the gown. He slipped out of his tux pants and laid the items neatly over the only chair.

In a moment they were undressed. He held the comforter up and let her climb in the bed. He clicked on a soft light and closed the door to the galley, then joined her, his arms enclosing her after he pulled the comforter over them. It was like being in a cocoon of warmth and safety.

The storm reached the cove and rocked the boat, sometimes gently, sometimes vigorously. The rain lashed the sea and all that floated upon it. But nothing penetrated the sweet wonder of their lovemaking.

Before they slept, he rose to turn off the light. For a few seconds, he stared down at her, his gaze fathoms deep, his thoughts unreadable as some emotion moved within his eyes and was gone.

Words rose to her lips, but she didn't say them. She wasn't sure what was allowed between lovers.

''Rest,'' he said gently, and kissed her eyes closed.

She let sleep take her as she rested secure in his arms. He'd been gentle, this sweet lover. For the moment, the yearning that had plagued her soul was quiet.

Chapter Two

Jean-Paul Augustuve, nineteenth Earl of Silvershire, zipped the final closure on the backpack.

"That's it," he said to his friend, Arnie Stanhope, who was also the expedition leader.

He and Arnie had been students together at Oxford and later at the University of Montana, where they'd studied archaeology. They were searching for remains of an ancient civilization here in the mountains of Silvershire.

Last month, a local shepherd had unearthed a burial chamber thought to be over fifteen thousand years old. Inside the mass grave site had been evidence of a ceremonial burial with food, weapons and other artifacts to aid the deceased in their afterlife. The discovery had tantalized scientists with the possibilities of finding a whole village and gaining insights into early man's way of life.

"When do you think you'll be back?" Arnie asked, running a hand through his hair, which was receding rapidly, giving him an oddly cherubic look with his round, smooth face and innocent expression.

Arnie, Jean-Paul had concluded long ago, was not of this world. Intensely involved in his exploration and research, he never noticed petty things about people, never lied or tried to impress anyone, was never impressed by a title or wealth. Arnie was just Arnie. Which was why Jean-Paul considered the scientist one of his best friends.

"I have no idea. When duty calls, I merely answer," he said with a rueful grin and shrug. He hoisted the backpack. "I'll be in touch."

"Are you sure you don't want a couple of men with you? It's a long trek out of the mountains."

"I'll be fine," Jean-Paul assured his friend. "Good luck with the dig."

They shook hands, and Jean-Paul left the campsite. Heading down the steep trail, he thought of the curious note tucked safely into his wallet. A ripple of some emotion he couldn't define ran over him.

Megan. Princess Megan Penelope Penwyck. The Quiet One. The sweet lover who had delighted him with her innocent passion. She'd been a virgin. That discovery had surprised him as much as the excited report of the shepherd on the ancient burial mound.

Her responsiveness had set him on fire, so much so he'd made love to her three times before morning came. They had both been silent on the voyage back to Monte Carlo.

For the first time in his life, he hadn't been able to summon glib conversation to ease the transition from the intimacy of the night to the casualness and eventual parting that came with the sunrise.

After the return to the hotel, he hadn't seen her again. She'd left for Penwyck the same day, slipping from the hotel without a word. He'd sent flowers to her home, but no note had answered the gift. He'd assumed the lady hadn't wanted a repeat of the night before.

His mood introspective, he paused on a summit that opened on a view of the castle and grounds several miles away from where he'd grown to manhood. He'd been caught up in state affairs, then the scheduled archaeological dig, for the past two months. There'd been no time to pursue the matter between him and the elusive princess from Penwyck.

The note he'd received yesterday had reminded him of her—concise and to the point. She'd requested a meeting with him at his earliest convenience.

That was it. No explanation, no references to the

past, no accusations, just the polite note penned in her own clear, precise handwriting.

However, it didn't take a genius to realize her request was dated eight weeks and one day after their night together.

Since their lovemaking had been totally unplanned, he hadn't had protection with him. However, he couldn't say he'd never thought of the possibility of a child. He had...and had ignored the precautions he always took when it came to involvement. Or entrapment.

As one touted by the tabloids as a Top Ten eligible bachelor, he was very careful about whom he dated and how involved their relationship became. Women with their own highly successful careers were sophisticated and just as leery of tying themselves down as he was.

A royal princess like Megan would have been taught from the cradle to be wary of the unexpected or impulsive. So how did either of them explain that one foolish but magical night they'd shared?

Unexpected and undefined emotion rushed over him. He studied it for a moment, then shrugged. Whatever would be, would be. *C'est la vie.*

The trip down the mountain took all of Tuesday and half of Wednesday. He had time to do a lot of soul-searching. Impending fatherhood didn't dismay him, he found.

It came to him that he was already thinking of it as a sure thing. If so, his parents would be pleased.

He had recently turned thirty, and they had given him several broad hints that it was time he, an only child, settled down and produced the required heir to Silvershire.

Perhaps he would surprise them with news of coming nuptials, he thought sardonically, entering the manse that served as the seat of his father's dukedom and which he would inherit one day. But not soon, he hoped.

He loved and admired his parents. Once he'd even assumed a passionate love would come to him as it had to them. Their marriage had been impulsive and had enraged his grandfather, the old duke. But it had worked out well.

Running up the stairs to his quarters, he knew word of his arrival—and his plans for immediate departure—would soon spread from the staff to the present duke. Hmm, what would he say about where he was going?

Tell the truth? He could be wrong about the child. Maybe the princess wanted to continue where they'd left off.

His body stirred to rigid life at the thought. He grimaced as he stripped, showered and changed into more formal clothing for the expected meeting with the duke and duchess. If he told his parents what he suspected, they would most likely have a marriage arranged for him before he could sail across the twenty-six miles to Penwyck and consult with the princess.

Heading down the steps, he decided it was better to keep his thoughts to himself, at least for now.

"Jean-Paul," his mother said, pausing in the hall and smiling up at him.

She was French and spoke English with an enchanting accent. Her hair and eyes were dark, her form petite. Daughter of a vintner with more family pride than money, she and his father had met in Monte Carlo, taken one look at each other and run off to Africa for a month before returning home to face the music.

Quickly descending the stairs, he suppressed thoughts of the strange but rapturous night when he'd also fled civilization and found his own magic land...

"Mother," he said, bending to kiss her on each cheek when he reached the marble entry hall. His heart gave a hitch of emotion as he smiled down at her.

"And what are you doing home? You found what you sought?" she demanded in her feisty-as-a-sparrow way.

For a second he considered confessing all, but realized he didn't really know anything.

"Something came up." He dropped an arm around her shoulders. "You look marvelous. Is that a new outfit?"

She slapped him on the arm. "You are not to distract me with fashion, which I, of course, adore.

What is this something that has come up? Or should a mother not ask?''

He grinned. ''Don't ask.''

''Then go greet your father in the library while I have another place set for lunch.''

She waltzed away, looking much younger than her years, and again his insides were tugged by unexpected emotion. He hurried toward the room his father used as an office and a family gathering place before meals.

He thought about asking his sire how he'd felt upon meeting the dainty Frenchwoman who had so taken his fancy and apparently his heart at their first glance.

But that might lead to other questions, and he had no answers, none at all....

''The king isn't available,'' the king's secretary said.

Jean-Paul suppressed a frown of irritation. ''Prince Bernier was assured King Morgan would see his emissary without delay.''

The secretary's pale, ascetic countenance didn't alter a fraction as he apologized again but offered no explanation for the postponement.

''When may I expect an audience?'' Jean-Paul demanded.

This time a flicker of emotion narrowed the cool gaze. Sir Selywyn spread his hands in an artful gesture that indicated his helplessness to set a date. ''I will contact you," he promised. "Are your quarters satisfactory?"

Jean-Paul considered the royal secretary about as helpless as a viper on a hot rock, but there was no point in pressing further. He'd been given quite adequate guest quarters in the royal palace, so he nodded, then left the office when Selywyn escorted him to the door, an obvious invitation to depart.

Standing in the great hall, used as a reception chamber and sometimes as a ballroom, Jean-Paul contemplated his next move. He'd done his duty for his liege, Prince Bernier of Drogheda, who'd asked him to fill in for the ambassador to Penwyck who'd taken ill. Now he'd have to wait on the whim of King Morgan for an appointment. Such were the affairs of state.

That left him free to pursue his prime reason for coming to Penwyck.

Megan.

He'd seen her as a young girl just entering the flower of womanhood in this very chamber at her sister's birthday ball. Ten years ago. Megan had been seventeen. He'd been twenty and much more worldly than the young girl he'd waltzed about the room.

His parents had insisted he attend the ball. They'd had an eye toward an alliance even then and had hoped he and Princess Meredith might form a tendresse for each other. He'd seen through their obvious ploy and kept his distance from the birthday princess.

There'd been no harm in flirting with the younger sister, though. Megan with the sun-kissed face and intriguing tan line on her throat that disappeared between her breasts, he recalled, then frowned at the heat that ran through his loins.

She'd admitted that she preferred walking along the shore to being here in the ballroom. Whirling her to the open terrace door, he'd then taken her hand and run with her through the formal gardens to a side gate. "Can you open it?" he'd asked.

"Of course."

She'd done so and led him through the family gardens to another gate, then down a sloping path along a cliff and thus to the sea. Kicking off their shoes, they'd walked along the strand for more than an hour, speaking only to indicate points of interest—seals sleeping on the breakwater rocks, the beam of a lighthouse keeping watch over the ships that plied the sea at night, palm trees growing along the secluded shore.

"The Gulf current brings warmth to the islands," he'd said, showing off his knowledge, "else we'd have a climate similar to Canada's, cold and snowy."

"I love the cove," she'd confided. "This was our private place to play and pretend and dream out of sight of the public, especially the news media."

She'd stopped as if embarrassed at complaining.

"It's hard having your every move watched, isn't

it?'' he'd said to put her at ease. ''Sometimes I want to escape, too.'' He'd surprised himself at the confession.

''But we can't. And we shouldn't dwell on it. Our lives are really very privileged.''

He'd frowned at her prim tone...until he'd looked at her. Her pose belied her words. She faced the sea, her eyes filled with longing so intense it had stunned him, as if something out there beyond his sight beckoned her.

''A selky,'' he'd murmured, stroking her hair. ''Trapped on shore in a human body. Do you long to return to the sea?''

''Yes,'' she'd said, her voice as sad as the call of a lonely gull.

At that moment, he'd wanted to pull her to him, to calm the urge that tugged her toward the sea, but he hadn't.

Washed in moonlight, her dress white and virginal, her eyes wild with grief for something that could never be, she'd seemed another being, ethereal and dangerous but mesmerizing the way the seal-folk were supposed to be. He'd been afraid to touch her more intimately.

But he'd wanted to, he admitted now with raw candor.

''How serious is it?'' Carson Logan, the king's personal bodyguard, demanded. ''When will he come out of it?''

The chief medical officer shook his head. "I can't predict the future. The king is in a coma. The question may not be *when* he'll come out of it but *if*."

Admiral Harrison Monteque cursed under his breath. "You *think* it's encephalitis? Don't you know?"

Head of one of the most highly trained intelligence organizations of modern times, the admiral was sharp, cunning and focused, well used to taking command.

The Royal Intelligence Institute, organized by the king to include the best minds in the fields of military, science, medicine, economics and such disciplines, was the envy of other leaders throughout the world. Operating inside this unique structure was the Royal Elite Team—men authorized to act in any emergency that threatened the kingdom or the Royal Family.

Admiral Monteque of the Royal Navy directed the RET. Duke Carson Logan was a member as was Sir Selywyn Estabon, the royal secretary, and Duke Pierceson Prescott. All four glared at the medical chief as if the king's condition was his fault.

The doctor glared back. "We're checking the diagnosis with the Center for Disease Control in the United States. This appears to be a rare strain of virus, found only in a limited area of Africa."

"How would the king contract such a disease?" Duke Prescott demanded.

"How the hell would I know?" the doctor snapped.

Sir Selywyn poured oil on troubled waters. "Please keep us informed the instant there's any change."

"Of course," the doctor replied stiffly. He hesitated, then added, "The body is a miraculous machine. The king could awaken and be right as rain at any moment. I will advise you of any improvement at once."

Selywyn escorted the doctor to the door of the king's council chamber, a room constructed so that no sound or electronic signal could escape or penetrate the barriers in its walls.

"We must proceed with all caution," Logan said after the secretary securely closed the door. "Until we know what is to happen with the king."

Monteque frowned. "It's the worst time—"

"Is there a best one?" Selywyn interrupted.

The two men locked gazes, then the admiral shrugged ruefully. "I suppose not. I think we shall have to proceed to Plan B, as we discussed last night."

"You were serious?" Logan questioned while Preston looked even grimmer.

"Dead serious. I don't see another choice, and it would be the king's wishes. Look at the situation. We're in critical negotiations with the United States on a trade agreement, in talks with Majorco on a military alliance and still have to convince the Ministers of the Exchequer of the wisdom of ratifying the international trade accord reached two months ago in Monaco. We must at least give the appearance of making progress on those fronts.''

Preston spoke up. ''The law says if the king becomes incapacitated, the queen takes over as regent until a royal son is crowned. What of her?''

''The queen has never shown much interest in political affairs. The King of Majorco's contempt for women entering a man's world is well-known. I suggest we stall, at least until we know what is to become of the king,'' Selywyn told them. ''Or until one of the royal princes returns to the country and is made king.''

Selywyn was aware of his own fatigue as Monteque rubbed a hand over his face in an unconscious gesture of weariness. None of them had slept for more than a couple of hours at a time since the king's mysterious ailment had befallen him last Sunday. It was now Thursday, and the military alliance treaty was to be signed in a public ceremony next month.

''It's a hell of a time for both Owen and Dylan to be out of the country and unavailable,'' Monteque continued. ''I don't think we should allow that in the future.''

''They're young men with minds of their own,'' Logan reminded the RET leader. He yawned and stretched. ''They won't be shackled.''

"Aye, the royals are different today than when the king and I were growing up," Monteque said, referring to the five royal children of King Morgan and Queen Marissa.

"But not, I think, in their hearts," Selywyn murmured. "I suppose we must get on with the business at hand. When should we put the emergency plan into effect, Admiral?"

Monteque rose. "At once."

The admiral, along with Preston, left the private chamber. Selywyn turned to his friend, Logan, who was as close to the king as he was. "I wonder if we are about to admit the Trojan horse into the kingdom."

But Logan's eyes were closed and his head nodded to one side. Selywyn touched the man's shoulder.

"Go to your bed, my friend," he told the king's bodyguard, who awoke with a start. "We'll all need our wits about us to see this through to the end."

Jean-Paul stood on the cliff that overlooked the private lagoon adjoining the grounds of the palace. His request for Megan to meet him had gone unanswered the previous day. Now he was taking matters into his own hands.

He felt certain she would slip down to her favorite place as soon as she had a spare moment, so he'd taken the liberty of going the long way to the shore, approaching the hidden cove along the strand from the northwest and staying well out of sight of the palace walls where he might be spotted by the ever-present surveillance cameras.

Glancing at his watch, he saw it was nearly noon. An early morning fog lingered over the bay. He'd been on the beach since seven, and his disposition was not improving as each minute ticked by.

A lone figure appeared out of the mist.

Ah. A smile tipped the corners of his mouth as he recognized the graceful form of Megan, Royal Princess of Penwyck, making her way down the rocky path along the cliffs. Patience was at last rewarded.

She walked with surefooted skill, a slight woman, no more than five feet, four inches, weighing hardly more than a hundred pounds. Her dark hair curled damply around her shoulders in the mist, its auburn highlights dimmed by the fog. She held a long shawl snugly around her to ward off the chill breeze from the ocean.

He decided not to call out to her until she was on the beach so as not to startle her. A thrum of anticipation beat through him like jungle drums from a distant place. He remembered vividly how she had whispered his name in wonder as he'd caressed her.

During those moments, while the storm surged around them, the wildness of the selky had returned to her eyes. She'd been incredibly passionate, responsive to his every touch, until he, too, had felt the call of the sea in his blood, until his heart had pounded with the fierceness of the storm surge, until he'd thought it would burst from his chest...

The next moment he exclaimed in annoyance as the princess skipped lightly over the rocks in the opposite direction from him rather than walking around the cove as he'd thought she would do. Some instinct cautioned him to silence as she approached the water's edge.

To his astonishment, she tossed off the long shawl and her sandals. Clad only in a swimsuit, she raced into the chill sea and proceeded to swim out into the bay on the morning tide.

Surprise was replaced by a surge of fear so strong he was rendered motionless for a split second. Then he was on his feet, tossing shoes and clothing aside, and diving into an oncoming wave, determined to haul her back to shore.

She was a surprisingly strong swimmer and she knew how to ride the outgoing tide to her advantage. She was almost abreast of a small rocky island centered in the bay when he caught up with her.

Her eyes opened wide in obvious shock upon discovering him when she glanced over her left shoulder. "Wha—" she began. "Who is it?" she demanded in true regal style.

He raised his head and looked at her.

Her eyes, as green as the sea could sometimes

be, stared at him as if he were a strange creature she'd never seen before. Anger joined the hunger and fear and all other emotions that filled him.

"Jean-Paul Augustuve," he informed her sardonically. "Good morning, Your Highness." He executed a bow.

But Megan had already discerned who he was, had known it instinctively upon spying the dark hair and long, lean figure closing in on her as she neared the island.

"Hello," she said in confusion.

Being that she was a virgin prior to her encounter with Jean-Paul, she'd never met an ex-lover face-to-face after the crime, so to speak. It was doubly awkward treading water while they spoke, like a couple of merfolk meeting accidentally. She had neither a mermaid's nor a worldly woman's wit and nonchalance.

"Hello, indeed." He stretched out and in two strokes had arraigned himself beside her.

She swam to the rocky shore of the island, Jean-Paul beside her all the way.

"You didn't answer my note yesterday," he said when they stood side by side, water sluicing from their bodies.

A bolt like lightning hit her when she realized he wore only underclothes that clung, almost transparent, to him like a second skin. She hurriedly turned and selected a boulder to perch on so she could watch the restless ocean.

"I was busy," she told him, groaning silently at how haughty she sounded.

"Which is why I waited for you here."

She shot him an assessing look, not sure of his mood. His manner was calm, but she sensed the danger he could be if he chose.

"How nice to see you," she said formally.

"Weren't you expecting me?"

She shook her head.

His laughter was brief. "Did you think I was a callow youth who would flee in the face of fatherhood?"

A gasp tore from her throat, which suddenly seemed too hoarse to speak. She hadn't had near enough time to prepare herself for this meeting, to find the words to ask what his intent might be, what his wishes were. "I...why do you say that?"

"A cryptic note that you needed to see me, written eight weeks and a day from our night on the sea? I would think it's fairly obvious what conclusion should be drawn."

"Oh."

His hands clenched at his sides. His eyes raked her in anger. She felt like cringing but managed not to.

"Are you expecting a child?"

His voice lashed at her, shocking her as much as the question. "If I am?" she asked to gain time.

"There is no need for panic." He gestured toward her and the sea. "I will do my duty toward you and the babe."

The words should have soothed her troubled heart, but she was only more confused. It came to her that he perhaps thought she was considering taking her life and that of the child. Resentment, anger and other emotions whirled through her. She lifted her chin as pride asserted itself. "I am hardly in a panic. I often come out to the island when I wish to be alone and think…about things."

Her hesitation must have given her away. "Then there is a child," he concluded.

"No," she denied.

He was silent while his eyes swept over her figure. "No?"

Her two-piece swimsuit suddenly seemed much too revealing. She opened her mouth, but no lie flowed from her lips. "I haven't seen a doctor yet," she confessed.

With a quick move, he caught her shoulders. "You said you didn't play games. Don't start with me," he warned.

She took a deep breath. "Then yes, I think I am…that there is…"

"I'll go to your father at once."

She stared into his clear blue eyes. He seemed to have no problem accepting this possibility at all. "Why?"

"To ask for your hand. We must follow protocol. After all, you are a royal princess."

"Wait," she said, laying a hand on his chest as if he might dash up the knoll and confront her father on the spot. "I must think."

Heat pulsed from where she touched him, running up her arm in waves that reminded her of the passion she'd found in his embrace. She pressed a hand to her temple, the world spinning completely out of control.

"We have some time," he conceded, "but it isn't infinite. Royal weddings take preparation. Or were you planning to elope?"

Now there was open amusement in his manner, as if he laughed at her expense.

"I wasn't planning anything," she informed him sharply, stepping away from his touch.

"I've heard pregnant women are often unreasonable," he remarked, his smile widening.

"I'm not unreasonable! You can't just waltz in here and start planning a wedding as if...as if..."

"As if we were lovers who'd been unable to wait for official blessings on our union?"

She stared at him aghast. He was twisting everything she said. And confusing her. Drawing courage around her like a cloak, she said, "I must go back. I have an appointment."

His smile said he knew she was lying, but he spoke quite gently. "We'll have dinner tonight and talk then. In the palace, or shall we go out?"

Everyone would notice if they went to a restaurant. Desperation seized her, and she said the first thing that came to mind. "In my chambers. I'll arrange it."

"Good." He guided them into the sea, staying by her side until they reached the mainland.

She kept her gaze carefully averted from the enticing flex of his muscles as they donned their garments. He escorted her to the palace gate, then lifted her chin with a finger and gazed into her eyes.

"Marriage to me may not be so bad as you obviously think," he suggested with a touch of bitterness.

She avoided his gaze. "We'll talk tonight. At eight." She unlocked the gate and fled, rushing to her chambers in a welter of undefined emotion. "Hurry," she said to her maid. "We have things to do."

Then she sank into a chair and sat there in a daze, doing nothing at all.

Chapter Three

Megan paced from her desk to the window, then started back. She paused in front of the hearth and considered ordering a fire. But that might be construed as too intimate. God forbid she appear eager for intimacy with the handsome Earl of Silvershire.

She would have laughed at the irony but she wasn't sure she'd be able to stop. *Poor princess,* everyone would say as they carried her away. *She just couldn't handle the affairs of state.*

It was affairs in general that she couldn't handle, she admitted with gallows humor.

An authoritative knock sounded at the door. Candy, her personal maid, hovering over the table set for two, glanced her way in question. Megan nodded and stayed at the hearth.

Jean-Paul entered, thanked the maid, then looked directly into Megan's eyes, trapping her with his commanding presence when she really wanted to bolt to her bedroom and hide in the closet. He bowed with careless grace.

Tonight he wore all black—slacks, shirt, sans tie, and velvet jacket. He looked like a storybook prince.

"You're beautiful," he said, as if this were such a simple truth it should be obvious to anyone who saw her.

Although the night often grew cool due to the sea breeze, she'd chosen a long summer dress of golden silk with satin leaves of deep green around the neckline and elbow-length sleeves and hem. He handed her a golden rose wrapped with ribbons of variegated green.

"Thank you. That was thoughtful." She slipped the wrist corsage over her left hand, staring at it in confused wonder.

"I called and asked Candy about your outfit," he explained.

An odd resentment flowed through her at the casual use of her maid's name. Then it was gone as she recalled the whisper of her own name on his lips. *Megan,* he'd said in a husky murmur that magic night. *Sweet selky.*

At that moment, had she been such a creature, she would never have traded her human form for that of the sea mammal, although selkies supposedly yearned to return to their watery home.

She was brought back to the present when Jean-Paul crossed the carpet and lifted her hand to his lips. His kiss was brief and formal. But only for a moment, then he turned her hand and kissed her wrist. She gasped.

The maid gave a surprised exclamation, then quickly coughed to cover it. When Megan frowned her way, the girl smoothed an imaginary wrinkle in the tablecloth.

"You may serve the first course," Megan said, sweeping past the earl and hearing the whisper of the silk against her thighs at the same instant she inhaled his scent, which was that of balsam cologne, shampoo and talc...and one she was thoroughly acquainted with.

She had to stop thinking like that!

"Please join me," she invited, stopping at the table, which, set for two, seemed much too confining. However, they could hardly discuss their problems at the family table.

Besides, her mother was filling in at some royal function for the king this evening and the twins were out of the country, so only the princesses were at home. Megan didn't want to share Jean-Paul with her sisters at present.

Thinking of the king, Megan wondered what important project had come up. Her father hadn't been seen the past five days. Neither Megan nor her sisters knew what was up, which was not unusual; their father had left the raising of the children to his queen while he attended royal affairs.

On second thought, Meredith, who worked with the Royal Intelligence Institute, might know, but she hadn't said.

Growing up in a palace, one learned to discern the faintest nuances of intrigue. Megan had discovered long ago that things were seldom as they seemed in a royal household and that personal matters always were last in priority. Her gaze went to her handsome guest.

"Deep thoughts?" Jean-Paul's smile was mocking but not sarcastic or cruel. She'd never seen him act in a mean-spirited manner, a good trait in a father.

Quickly, before her unruly mind went off on another tangent, she sat and arranged her skirts while he took the chair opposite her. Candy served a chilled plum soup from fruit grown on the royal farm. Megan saw Jean-Paul's eyes linger on the girl, a frown in the blue depths.

"That will be all for the evening, Candy," Megan told the maid. "We'll serve ourselves."

With a confused bow, the young woman, recently turned eighteen, left the sitting room.

"Alone at last," her guest murmured, his face relaxing into a pleased expression.

Startled at the laughter in his eyes, she managed a smile and picked up her spoon. The meal was consumed in near silence. She was glad she'd chosen only four courses, for she couldn't come up with a topic of small talk, and he didn't try.

After they finished the white chocolate mousse, they returned to the sitting area. He chose the sofa after she took a chair at right angles to it.

She poured him a cup of coffee, black with no sugar as she remembered from their week in Monte Carlo, then prepared her own with half milk and one spoon of sugar.

"What is your position on marriage?" he asked as soon as the formalities were complete.

The question shook her composure like a broadside hitting a sailing ship. "I don't approve of arranged ones."

A frown snapped a groove between his eyes. "Has one been proposed for you?"

The fury startled her. "No. Of course not. Meredith would be wed first."

He leaned forward and rested his forearms on his thighs. "Life as a royal is damned difficult. I suppose we would need to spend most of the year here. That wouldn't be a problem while my father is alive. When I inherit, we'll have to spend at least half the time at Silvershire."

"This is absurd," she began. He was planning where they would live while she hadn't yet come to terms with a possible marriage.

His eyes met hers in a brilliant glance of blue fire. "You'll like it there. We have the sea and the mountains just as you do here. I'll show you my secret places.''

"Wait!" she cried softly. "You're...this is going too fast. I haven't told my parents yet."

"I said I'd speak to your father. Do you think I'd let you take the heat alone?"

"That's noble of you, but as you noted, there's no need to rush into anything."

"Yet," he added, his gaze sweeping over her. "You're small. A child will show soon. Have you been ill in the mornings?"

She nodded, shy about admitting it. The fact seemed more intimate than the night they'd shared.

"And there is this," he murmured, continuing his train of thought.

His move took her off guard as he gathered her into his arms, then easily lifted her to his lap. His lips touched her cheek, then followed a line down to her mouth when she dared look at him.

"I should reprimand you," she told him sternly, but the scolding was for herself, for wanting his kiss.

"Are you going to?" he asked, not pausing in the light skimming touches of his lips on hers.

"No. I'm as wicked as you."

He stopped, then laughed. "I'll have to get used to your honesty."

She laid a hand on his chest inside his jacket. "Do you deal only with dishonest women?"

"Perhaps. Or only with those who are very practiced at dissembling."

The cynical admission reminded her that his life had been spent in the public eye much as hers had. Another bond, she thought and wondered how many more might be formed between them...and if that was good or bad for the heart.

He stroked her arms through the thin silk. "I've missed the taste of you. One night wasn't enough."

"How many would be?"

Raising his head, he studied her with a certain tinge of hostility in his gaze. "Where did that come from?"

She met his eyes levelly. "You. You've lived a liberal existence. Would one woman please you?"

He deftly rose and set her on her feet. "Perhaps. If she is the right woman." His eyes pierced the thin ice that surrounded her heart. "And if I so choose."

Megan managed not to flinch in the face of his cool statement of truth. She even smiled, because that magic night she'd let herself dream of their falling in love and sharing a true fairy-tale romance. But that was fantasy. Reality was having lunch and hearing her sisters speculate on the handsome Earl of Silvershire.

"Perhaps he seeks a bride," Anastasia had suggested with irrepressible humor. "Which shall he choose—the brain, the nun or the jock?"

They had mocked the news media by choosing

nicknames among themselves, a secret bit of foolishness for their own amusement. Owen was referred to as the cowboy and Dylan was the captain due to his fascination with the sea and pirates. Only among the royal five did they use these names.

Megan sighed. At lunch, a desire to confide all to her sisters had nearly overwhelmed her. However, first she must speak with her father. No. First she would speak to her mother. The queen would know what to do.

Jean-Paul's expression softened fractionally. "It has always been my intention to be true to my wife. Is that your only worry?" he demanded imperiously.

She ignored the question. "My sisters wondered if you came seeking a bride."

"Did you tell them that choice was made?"

"Forced, you mean." Her shoulders slumped. "How could we have been so foolish?"

She meant it as a rhetorical question, but he answered anyway. "What mortal can resist a selky?"

He hooked a finger under her chin and lifted her face to his. For a long second those icy blue eyes delved into hers, making her hot instead of cold.

"An alliance between us would work out well." He paused as if in deep thought. "If you don't want the baby, I will take it. My mother would love to have a grandchild to spoil."

"I would never give up my child!"

His manner became frigid. "Neither would I. We

may have behaved foolishly, but the little one had no part in that. We must do what is best for his or her future." He released her and walked toward the door. "Think upon that."

She was speechless as he left her apartment. He wanted the child and thought she didn't?

Wrapping her arms across herself, she contemplated the future. A child, she mused in wonder. A child that came from a magical night. And she knew who the selky had been in that wonderful coming together...

Queen Marissa turned her head at the sound of approaching footsteps. "Oh," she said softly, surprised.

Her husband of thirty years, King Morgan, stopped, picked a red rose, removed the thorns and came to her.

Heart suddenly thudding, she watched him with a wary stance. She hadn't seen him in over a week. Which wasn't unusual. It was the way of a royal marriage.

She'd been twenty-three to his twenty-eight when they'd wed. An arranged marriage, of course, conducted through officials and ambassadors. Courtship had taken place after the wedding.

A blush lightly warmed her cheeks as she recalled that wondrous honeymoon.

As if he, too, were swept back into a distant time, Morgan bowed before her. With a slight smile on his handsome face, he reached out with the long-stemmed rose and lightly drew it along her cheek, its cool petals like damp satin against her skin. He then continued down her throat until finally he paused at the vee of her morning gown.

With a deft movement, he tucked the flower between her breasts. Heat spread to a point deep inside her. She searched his face, not sure of the meaning of the rose. She saw passion in his eyes and felt an answer in herself. It had been such a long time...

Finally he sighed and retreated a step. "I must be going," he said, "but I saw you in your garden and knew I couldn't ignore such beauty."

She studied the paleness of his skin. No matter how busy he was, he usually took time for brisk walks during the day. "You've been working very hard of late," she began, then stopped, not wanting him to think she was complaining.

"And will be doing so in the future," he added with a grimace. "Matters of state demand long hours."

He lifted one finger to his mouth, then touched her lips, implanting a kiss there. A thrill went through her as if she were a young bride just getting to know her husband.

"I will see you...soon," he murmured, his eyes hot, almost feverish, as he bid her farewell.

It took her a moment to get her breath after he

disappeared inside the palace. A knock on the outside garden door caused her to start and gasp.

"Mother?" called the voice of her middle daughter. "May I come in?"

"Please do," she answered, composing herself.

Megan entered and closed the door carefully behind her. She executed a perfect curtsy, then came
forward. Marissa noted her second child's hesitant
air and immediately put her own worries aside.

"How lovely you look," she said, patting the
bench beside her under the old rose arbor. "It
seems ages since I've seen you."

Megan settled herself, paying much attention to
arranging the skirts of her morning gown. "We've
all been busy of late."

Contrition ate at Marissa's conscience. She and
the king had so little time for their children any-
more. The girls had their own interests and the
twins loved adventuring around the world.

"You seem worried," she said, giving the girl
an opening gambit.

Megan nodded, not sure how to begin. "When
you and father were married, did he love you?"

She watched her mother anxiously and held in
all the words that ached to tumble from her tongue
in a surfeit of confession, guilt and uncertainty.

"I..." The queen stared at her in confusion, then
an understanding smile curved the corners of her
mouth. "Are you in love, my darling?"

Megan blinked back the sting of tears. She shrugged.

"Might I ask with whom?"

"It wasn't love," Megan said after a long silence. "I mean…I don't think…I'm not sure…"

Her mother touched her hand lightly, comfortingly. "Tell me what I can do to help?"

Megan stared at the rose tucked into her mother's gown. "You and Father love each other, but your marriage was arranged. Did you fall in love before the marriage? Or afterward?"

Megan saw she'd totally stunned her mother, who reddened then went pale. She swallowed and tried to think of words to explain to her parent the welter of feelings that darted around inside her without rhyme or reason.

"You are in love," the queen said softly.

"No! That is, there is someone—" Megan realized she was going to have to tell her mother the bare facts at the very least if she were to ask for advice.

"Who?"

"Jean-Paul Augustuve of Silvershire," Megan answered.

"Jean-Paul," her mother repeated. She frowned. "His bloodline is acceptable, but he is known as something of a rebel. Your father may not be pleased."

"There is another problem."

"Yes?"

"There is a child."

"Jean-Paul has a child?"

Megan didn't blame her mother for looking confused. "Not yet."

"I don't think I understand."

"I am with child," Megan said in a low voice, as if the stone walls around the queen's private garden had ears.

Her mother clasped both hands to her bosom. She lifted the rose from between her breasts and stared at it as if the flower might interpret this news for her.

"Jean-Paul's child," the queen concluded.

Megan nodded and sighed as a weight lifted slightly from her shoulders. Her mother was quick to catch on. She was also thoughtful. Megan was grateful the older woman didn't push a lot of questions at her, but instead contemplated the rose with an enigmatic smile hovering on her lips.

"Tell me what you can," her mother invited.

"You recall I went to Monaco for the trade conference in Meredith's place in April?"

Megan related the facts: Jean-Paul had been there, too. She'd noticed him. They'd spoken a few times. He'd complimented her speech before the conference. She finally got to the night aboard his sailing yacht.

"And?" her mother prompted.

"And nothing. I mean, we haven't agreed upon anything."

The queen's eyes narrowed dangerously. "Does he not wish to marry?"

"He says we must. Because of our positions." Megan stood, her hands clenched, and strode about the flagstones. "I will not accept that kind of marriage. Look at what happened to Prince Charles and Princess Diana."

"Aye," murmured the queen. "A tragic waste."

"How did you and Father make it work?"

Her mother again stared at the rose she held. "Sometimes luck plays a part, I suppose. Both parties have to want a good marriage. Your father and I did. I wouldn't let him close me out. I went to him, quite shamelessly, I must admit, during those early years." She smiled in womanly conspiracy.

Megan smiled, too, even as she blushed.

"Tell Jean-Paul what you want from him," the queen advised. "And use the attraction between you to cement the bond that already exists. Insist that he help with the child. That is another bond."

Megan took a deep breath and squared her shoulders. Everything seemed much simpler now that she'd talked with her mother. "What of Father? Shall I tell him right away?" she asked.

Marissa frowned thoughtfully. "The king is extremely busy at present. Perhaps you and Jean-Paul should work things out to your satisfaction, then speak to the king."

"Should Jean-Paul ask for my hand?" Megan rolled her eyes. "That sounds so outdated."

Her mother laughed and gave her a little hug. "I will give a private dinner in my apartments when you are ready. The two of you may tell the king then, in whatever manner you decide. As old-fashioned as it sounds, I think your father would be delighted if Jean-Paul formally asked for your hand. As soon as he gets over being furious."

Megan hugged the queen back. "Thank you. I knew you would know what to do. I will advise you as soon as Jean-Paul and I have talked."

Marissa watched her daughter walk quickly from the garden, heading for the shore path and the cove where Megan went to think and be alone just as she used the private rose garden for her own haven. For a moment she regretted the loss of her sweet little girl, the Quiet One, who'd watched the world with her solemn green eyes and kept her thoughts to herself.

"Please," she prayed for her child, "let her be happy. Let there be love."

She sat on the bench while the bees hummed over the flowers and wished for all the desires of the heart for the royal princess.

And for her own heart?

Staring at the rose Morgan had given her that morning, she had to admit she didn't know. They had drifted apart, each intent on his or her duties, over the past few years, but that could change... perhaps already had.

Her heart gave a hitch. The way he'd looked at

her, stroked the rose over her skin, those had to mean something. Could they recapture their early years together? Could they find joy and passion again?

For a moment she was filled with longing and a glimmer of the possibilities. The mood faded. No one could have everything, she concluded with a sigh. Not a princess or a queen.

Especially not a queen.

Chapter Four

Megan snipped the dead heads off the prize dahlias, aware of the gardener's disapproving eyes on her the whole time. These were the royal family's private gardens, but he considered all the palace grounds, both public and private, to be his personal domain. She ignored him.

Jean-Paul had been in residence since Wednesday. Three days and all the females in the Penwyck capital city of Marlestone were atwitter over the handsome earl. The gossip and speculation about him set her teeth on edge.

Her maid had updated Megan on his activities. He'd appeared briefly at a local night spot late last night after leaving her. He didn't dance with anyone although one bold female had asked him; he'd good-naturedly bought her and all her friends an ale, then left soon after. This morning, he had rented a motorbike and raced along the beach, a popular Saturday endeavor. Several local young men had joined him, and a good time was had by all. Or so Megan heard.

Huffing in exasperation, she wondered where he was at the present. She'd requested a meeting that morning to discuss the future and the queen's invitation for an intimate dinner to inform her father of their plans. He'd left her stewing without an answer while he followed his own pursuits. Just as she'd done him the day he'd arrived.

Snip. Snip.

She slashed the drooping heads of two spent flowers, accidentally getting a third, healthy one. She quickly looked around to see if old Pierre, the gardener, was watching. He was.

He glared at her from the rose arbor tucked next to the high stone wall surrounding the family gardens.

Megan ducked her head and pretended not to see his scowls. *Snip. Snip.* She decapitated another dahlia, then realized she'd cut a second perfect bloom off in its prime.

Pierre muttered direly in French.

Disgusted with herself, she tossed her basket of cuttings into the compost bin and stored her gloves and shears in the potting shed. After wiping her face

and hands with a damp towel, she strolled the man-
icured paths until she came to a favorite spot by
the back wall that overlooked the cove.

Using a stone bench in a hidden niche behind a
birch tree as a stepping stool, she perched on the
wall and looked out at the sea.

The restless march of the waves on the shore
taunted her queasy stomach. She quickly looked
away from the sea to the hills that undulated in deep
swells to finally become the Aronleigh Mountains
stretching up the western coast of the country.

Two figures sauntered along the path leading
over the moors. As she watched, they paused and
studied a flower blooming among the heather.

Jean-Paul and a woman.

When he moved aside, Megan recognized the
blond hair and slender figure of Amira Corbin,
daughter to the queen's favorite lady-in-waiting and
chief confidante. He plucked the flower and tucked
it behind the girl's ear.

Megan heard the laughter of the younger female
as she spun away and dashed down the pathway,
her manner carefree and easy. Amira stopped and
pointed out another interesting tidbit to her handsome companion.

Resentment burned briefly in Megan's breast,
then was gone. The emotion wasn't allowed.

As a royal, she and her siblings had never been
permitted the kind of freedom that was taken for
granted by others. A guard would have followed

her had she left the palace compound or cove directly below. She'd learned long ago to quit fighting the restraints of her position.

Turning back to the sea, she experienced an intense longing to fling herself into its ever-shifting embrace and follow it to foreign shores and exotic lands, never to return....

She sighed and let her shoulders slump. She never gave in to her wilder impulses. Except for once.

Laying a hand against her roiling tummy, she sighed again. The king would be furious when she and Jean-Paul confessed all. He was very strict on protocol and the duty of the royals to set a good example.

Dear heaven, how could she have been so foolish that one night? What had she been thinking?

Now she would be forced into the very thing she'd always dreaded: an arranged marriage with no real feeling in it. Jean-Paul seemed to have accepted their fate, but she hadn't. There must be another way—

Laughter interrupted the berating of herself. Amira and the earl entered the family gardens. Megan heard them discussing the merits of the various blooms.

"Behold the dandelion," Jean-Paul said, stopping several feet away from Megan's niche. "It asks for nothing but a tiny wedge of soil tucked into a crevice of the wall. Its needs are modest—

no water but nature's own tears, no fertilizer but that of the good earth, and no tending by any hand but that of the sun.''

''Ah, but once this bloom has crept inside, it blows its seeds thither and yon,'' Amira responded gaily, ''and soon takes over the garden, allowing no space for more delicate blossoms.'' She pulled the plant out by the roots and tossed it over the wall.

Megan saw the plant spin over the cliff and fall to the sea. She, too, felt like an intruder in Eden.

But no, she wasn't the weed in this paradise. Jean-Paul was a guest in her country and her home. He chose to ignore *her* and play the gallant with another.

Lifting a loose pebble from the wall, she clenched it in her fist and fought an urge to fling it at the couple. However, it wasn't large enough to do damage and so would only be a sop to her pride, she decided grumpily.

''I must go,'' Amira said regretfully. ''Duty calls.''

''Then you must answer.''

Then you must answer, Megan mouthed, lifting her chin contemptuously at the honeyed tones. What a practiced rake he was!

When he bowed over the girl's hand, Megan couldn't restrain a soft snort, which was safely hidden in the sound of the sea and the wind. Amira twirled away with an attractive toss of her long blond tresses.

Megan hadn't realized Lady Gwendolyn's daughter was such a flirt. Perhaps she should warn the girl's mother to have a chat with her daughter about the perils of becoming involved with handsome strangers.

Not that Jean-Paul was a true stranger. In fact, her family had known his forever. The old kings of Penwyck, Drogheda and Majorco once tried to conquer each other just as those of England, Ireland and Scotland did.

But those were ancient days. This was now. And she was no nearer to solving the question of her babe's future than she'd been since penning that note to him.

In a fury she flung the stone from her hand, then stifled a gasp as it hit Jean-Paul squarely in the back. Holding her breath, she hoped he wouldn't notice or would attribute the assault to an insect blowing in the wind.

Slowly, leisurely, he turned toward the wall and her secret lair. A devilish grin appeared on his face.

"You have no reason for jealousy, Your Highness," he called out softly so that old Pierre, fussing around the dahlias half the garden's length away, wouldn't hear. "I was on my way to see you." He lifted a birch branch and entered her leafy grotto.

At once she erased any emotion from her face.

Squaring her shoulders, she informed him, "I would hardly be jealous of a girl. Amira is only twenty."

He looked back to where the younger woman disappeared into the wide door at the rear of the palace, then swung around to face her, a mysterious smile on his face.

His eyes were bluer than the sky as they caught the morning sunlight in their depths. His hair was a rich brown like semisweet chocolate. A few silver threads intruded here and there in the slightly wavy tresses. Again he was dressed in black—boots, jeans and shirt.

A rebel, she mused. That was his reputation. Bold among the ladies, too. He could also be incredibly gentle.

"A pence for them," he said, reaching out to touch her lightly at the temple.

"You'd be shortchanged."

Laughing, he nodded in acknowledgment of her quip, then said, "You sent for me?"

He stepped on the bench, then sat close to her on the wall. His scent wafted around her, as fresh as the morning.

"I spoke to my mother," she began, and stopped.

"Queen Marissa," he said in an encouraging manner. "She's as beautiful as her daughter."

"My mother is beautiful. I am not."

"You don't see yourself as others do."

Megan frowned. It seemed vain to argue her

looks with him. "She has offered to entertain the king with a private dinner when...when we are ready to tell him our news."

"Of our marriage?" Jean-Paul asked easily.

"Of the child."

"Hmm, knowing my own dear pater, I suggest we approach marriage first and the reasons later."

"What are the reasons?" She dared challenge him with her gaze when he cast her a direct stare.

Finally he shrugged. "The child, assuming there is one. Have you seen a doctor?"

She shook her head.

"We should do that. Is there one you trust?"

"Of course. The royal doctor is discreet." She folded her hands in her lap to conceal their trembling. "What other reason is there for the marriage?"

"The scandal that would be created should the story break before we're prepared to face it." He laid a hand on her arm and stroked back and forth. "My father would be in a fury if that should happen. I imagine yours would be, too, would he not?"

She nodded unhappily.

"There's the passion," he continued. His lips curved ever so slightly into a smile that mocked them both. "I want to make love to you each time I see you. I think you feel the same."

His fingers closed around her wrist where her pulse hammered away, making denial useless. She pulled away from his tempting touch.

"We could give free rein to that," he said.

She thought of other royal marriages, so romantic in the press, so dismal in reality. "While it lasted," she murmured sadly. "Then we would be tied to each other for all time. I don't approve of divorce."

The smile fled his face and was replaced with cool anger. "You should have thought of that before you leaped aboard my ship."

The words stung, but she held on to her pride and nodded her head crisply.

"The marriage would be good from the standpoint of both countries."

"Perhaps," she agreed, "but I've not made up my mind to it. I could go away—"

Her shoulders were seized roughly. "You will not destroy the child. I will not permit it."

"No, no," she said. "I wouldn't. I simply meant there are places I could go, a sojourn out of the country to study abroad until the child is born. That's what I meant."

"Then what?"

"Removed from the throne, the scandal would soon die. I wouldn't deny the child's heritage, but if we maintained a low profile, so to speak, people would cease to comment."

He eased his grip, but didn't release her. "Marriage would solve all our problems."

"Would it?"

Jean-Paul studied his reluctant bride's downcast face. Marriage to him certainly ranked far down on her list of priorities, that much was clear. So much for his reputation as a world-class lover.

But he had pleased her. And she had more than pleased him. It had been a night to remember, filled with her sighs and little moans of delight and a passion that had flared as brightly as an exploding star.

"What do you want that I cannot supply?"

"I'd thought to marry for love." She ducked her head as if embarrassed by her sentiment, then raised her chin to stare at him defiantly.

The simplicity of her statement, coupled with the hopelessness of her tone, enraged him for reasons he couldn't name. Bah, she lived in a storybook, and he had no patience for pretense.

"So you do play games, after all," he muttered. "You want sweet words and whispered lies—"

"No!" She half turned her back on him and stared out at the sea. "I told you—I want nothing from you. I got myself into this. I will handle it."

Flames erupted deep inside. "You didn't do it alone. I played my part...too well, it seems. I will not deny the child to your parents or mine."

"Perhaps it isn't yours."

Her challenges and denials threatened his control. He fought the fury. "It's mine. You were a virgin in my arms, and I have the proof aboard the ship."

She stared at him aghast, a furious blush highlighting her face.

He laughed softly as memories surfaced, routing

anger with tenderness and delight. "You were inexperienced, Princess. I was not."

"You don't know what has happened since that night, or with whom."

Her lie was absurd, her defiance maddening. "Show me your greater knowledge," he dared, and pulled her to his chest.

He took her startled mouth and smothered the tiny cry as he sought her sweetness. Her lips were like honey and he fed as eagerly as a bee among the honeysuckle vines.

The stiffness of her slight frame was a challenge in itself. He lifted her to his thighs.

His erection was already hard against his belly, and she moved against it instinctively, sending hot licks of fire throughout his body. He groaned and snuggled his face into her hair, fighting the need to make love to her right there, no matter the consequences.

"Your body answers mine," he murmured, planting kisses along her temple while his hands roamed of their own accord along her back and thighs.

"It's only lust."

"That, my prim princess, is quite enough. For now," he added. "Marriage and children would bring their own bonds."

"I will not marry for your convenience, nor for the sake of protocol."

He lifted her chin so he could study her mulish

expression. "Thus far I've found very little to be convenient in my dealings with you, Megan of Penwyck. I have answered when you called, leaving exploration that was important to me for others to discover. I've danced to your tune since arriving in your fair land. I hold my baser instincts in abeyance out of consideration for your tender feelings, although your body demands my attention—"

"That is not true!"

He flicked the pointed tip of her enticing breast. "What is this? A chill? The day is pleasant, not cold."

She gasped and crossed her arms, denying him the treasure that belonged to him.

"Stop being childish and accept the fate that has been preordained for us," he ordered, giving her a severe frown to keep from kissing her again.

Before he realized what she was doing, she leaped out of his arms and was gone, ducking beneath the tree branches and running along the garden path to disappear inside.

He had to remain in place. His condition would be all too evident to anyone he happened to meet. With his current luck, that would be the king or the queen, or both.

Forcing his thoughts to things cold in nature—glaciers, ice fields and Arctic blizzards—he cooled his blood, then followed the path to the palace family quarters where he was to dine. Perhaps he should speak to Queen Marissa.

But all thoughts of confession evaporated when he entered the library where the family gathered. Megan was there, looking as frosty and composed as a snow princess.

Beginning with the queen, he lightly held each lady's hand and called her by name, "Your Majesty, Lady Gwendolyn, Princess Meredith, Princess Megan, Princess Anastasia," he intoned, going to Megan, then Anastasia last, as protocol demanded.

Megan's green gaze mocked him when he finished his duties. He met her gaze levelly and determined not to let the fair selky disappear into the sea.

Megan was intensely aware of Jean-Paul hovering at her side like a persistent bumblebee among the dahlias as he chatted with the queen. She cast a searching glance at her mother when the queen asked him to sit at her right and Megan to sit beside him. The queen smiled blandly at her.

Once more Megan questioned her reasoning the night she had followed him aboard his sailing yacht....

"What?" she blurted, realizing everyone was looking at her.

"Lady Gwendolyn expressed an interest in the international trade conference," the queen said. "Perhaps, since both Jean-Paul and you attended, you could enlighten us on the proceedings there."

Megan's mind went totally blank.

"Accord was reached in several areas," Jean-Paul said smoothly, distracting attention from her. "The princess and I discussed an open-trade agreement between Drogheda and Penwyck during the week."

Megan stared at him, unable to recall such a conversation at all.

"Did you now?" the queen asked with a certain sardonic twist to the words.

Megan thought her mother sounded amused. She caught a smiling glance between Queen Marissa and Lady Gwendolyn. A horrible thought occurred to her: perhaps her mother had shared her news with her friend. But no, the queen was very good with confidences.

"But only in the most general terms," Jean-Paul added diplomatically. "It would be up to the ministers of each country to set the policies and present them to King Morgan and Prince Bernier."

"But of course," the queen agreed. "I'm sorry Amira couldn't join us. I believe she showed you the gardens this morning?"

"Yes," he said. "We walked out on the moors, too. The heather reminds me of Silvershire."

"Prince Bernier has sent you on several missions of late. Do you miss your home while you are gone?"

Jean-Paul smiled, his teeth brilliant against the tan of his skin. "The people more than the land," he said softly. "My parents and I are close. My uncle, the prince, visits our home frequently."

"Family is important to you then," the queen concluded.

"Yes."

Megan nearly jumped when his hand touched her arm and followed it to her hand. He took her hand in his under cover of the table and held it as if to reassure her of his honorable intentions toward her and the child.

A riot of emotion dashed around inside her like a robin chasing a butterfly. Flames licked her insides, whether from remembered passion or embarrassment, she couldn't decide.

Jean-Paul held her hand until the next course was served, then released it so she could lift her fork. She ate without tasting a morsel of the meat pie and tender summer vegetables. By the time fruit and cheese were served, she thought of nothing but escape. Her sister, Meredith, watched her from across the table with a perplexed expression in her eyes. Megan looked at her plate as much as possible.

"Jean-Paul, will you join me for tea in my sitting room?" Queen Marissa asked when the meal was finished.

Megan stared at her mother in alarm, but the queen only smiled gently and slightly shook her head, indicating Megan's presence was not required. Swallowing her fears, Megan left the room with her sisters and the lady-in-waiting.

After Lady Gwendolyn wished them good day and left the three girls in the royal family's sitting room, Meredith turned on Megan.

"What is going on?" she demanded.

"What?" asked Anastasia, confused by the question. If the conversation didn't include her beloved horses, she paid little heed to it. She was most like the king in temperament and athletic ability.

"Nothing," Megan replied to Meredith.

"What?" Anastasia asked again, realizing that more was going on than met the eye.

Meredith ignored the youngest sister, her eyes on Megan. "There is something between you and Jean-Paul," she accused. "He covered for you when your thoughts were obviously elsewhere. I think he held your hand at one point. You and he did more than discuss trade agreements while you were in Monte Carlo."

Heat suffused Megan's face as her sisters watched her with avid interest. "It's nothing," she said, but her voice quavered so even Anastasia detected the lie.

"What is going on?" she now demanded.

Meredith laughed in delight. "Our quiet Megan and the Earl of Silvershire are having an affair."

"No!" Megan denied. "It was only the one ni—" She clamped a hand over her mouth.

"Ah," said Meredith in satisfaction.

"Oh," said Anastasia in shock.

"One night," Meredith concluded. "And now he

has followed you to Penwyck. Does Mother know? Is that why she speaks to him in private?"

"Has he come to ask for your hand?" asked Anastasia, ever the romantic.

Megan slumped onto the sofa, refusing to answer.

Meredith looked pleased. "When are you thinking to marry?"

"I'm not!" Megan said sharply, then briefly laid a hand on her sister's arm in apology. "That is, I haven't made up my mind to it."

"Why ever not?" Anastasia asked. "He is handsome and exciting. All the palace maids are talking about him. Oh, you do not love him," she said as if just realizing this possibility. She shook her head at Megan. "You'd be foolish to turn down his offer."

"Our brothers will have no choice, and I, as the eldest daughter, may have to marry for duty," Meredith declared loftily, "but Megan needn't. She must follow her heart."

Megan sat in miserable silence while her sisters discussed the situation. The three princesses had spoken of their future marriages many times and speculated on which of the world's noble families might supply their future mates.

All three had vowed to marry only for love.

Reality, Megan was discovering, could be entirely another thing. If Jean-Paul offered and her father insisted, then she, too, would marry where told.

Would it be without love?

Her heart set up a terrible pounding so that she had to press a hand against her chest to ease its ache. If not for love, why had she allowed that night with Jean-Paul? She had no answer. Another question came to her: Why had he let her aboard his sailing retreat? He was a man of the world. Why had he succumbed to that mad passion?

"Tell us all," Meredith commanded with a queenly air.

"There is nothing to tell," Megan told her sisters. "Not yet, at any rate." She held up a hand in promise. "I will tell you as soon as there is."

Anastasia spoke to Meredith. "There is something."

"I told you," Meredith said, nodding wisely.

Megan laughed, overcome by the absurdity of it all. "I promise you will be among the first to know."

"Has he asked you to marry him?" Anastasia asked, stars in her eyes.

"Marriage has been mentioned," Megan admitted.

"Do you want the marriage?" Queen Marissa asked, studying the young man who had taken her daughter's innocence…and her love?

"It would have certain advantages."

She stifled impatience with the diplomatic answer. "Do you love her?"

The blunt question took him by surprise, bringing his gaze to her. She saw the quickly masked anger at her impertinent question.

"I would be a considerate husband," he assured her.

Sighing, she gazed out the window at the sea. "I would have romance and enchantment for my children. Perhaps that is impossible, a mother's foolish wish."

A smile briefly touched his handsome face. "There was magic," he said softly.

Her heart clenched, and she was filled with longing for the early days of her marriage to Morgan and the magic she'd found with him. Glancing at the large tome lying on the table, she shivered delicately as she recalled the pressed rose it held and how its petals had raked gently over her skin. At that moment, her husband of thirty years had seemed a different man.

"I would not have her hurt," she said.

"Neither would I." It was a promise.

Marissa nodded and offered her hand, dismissing the young man so that she could consider her daughter's future and pursue her own thoughts in private.

Chapter Five

Jean-Paul was escorted into the office of Admiral Harrison Monteque precisely at three. After the morning discussion with Megan and the one after lunch with the queen, he wasn't expecting a lot from the diplomatic meeting with the head of Penwyck's military forces.

Intelligence sources from his own county suspected Monteque was also head of a secret, elite force that reported only to King Morgan. However, this was conjecture since they had no hard evidence of such a group even existing.

Just as he had no real evidence of Megan's pregnancy. More than one man had been trapped by a female's wiles. Except Megan practiced no wiles.

She was as straightforward as any man he'd ever known. His best friend, Arnie Stanhope, would like her—

"Good afternoon," Monteque said, interrupting the odd tangent his thoughts had taken.

"Admiral," he responded.

"Please, be seated." The admiral waited until Jean-Paul was comfortably situated. "Coffee? Tea?"

"Neither, thank you." Jean-Paul studied the older man, noting the alert intelligence behind the pleasant mien and feeling the keenness in the man's glance.

"What can I do for you?" the admiral inquired, settling back in his own chair as if he had all the time in the world.

"Penwyck is about to enter a military alliance with Majorco," Jean-Paul stated.

The admiral nodded, disclosing nothing.

"Drogheda might be interested in joining such an alliance. Three small island nations would be more effective as a military force than one, or even two. There is still a certain safety in numbers."

"Why should Drogheda desire such an alliance? Your country has the full authority of the United Kingdom behind you. Behind them is their ally, the Americans."

"With which Penwyck is negotiating a trade and arms sales agreement, are you not?" Jean-Paul put in coolly.

Monteque's gaze sharpened to spear points, but he ignored the question. "Penwyck has the most up-to-date equipment and research facilities in the world. What would we gain by an alliance?"

"There would be advantages to your country as well as mine in the arrangement. Our balance-of-trade exchange with the rest of the world is excellent, as you must know. An open-trade agreement would be to your benefit. Morgan's emissary to the international trade conference mentioned that. Prince Bernier would consider it."

"Princess Megan," the admiral murmured, mentioning the emissary by name. "She went in Meredith's place."

Jean-Paul detected a slight change in tone and wondered what the admiral found significant in that fact. He knew Princess Meredith acted as liaison to the Royal Intelligence Institute for her father, the king. Was she supposed to have done something more during the conference than Megan had? Or that Megan had neglected to do?

"And handled her tasks very well," he said, worry eating at him for Megan's sake. He would not have it said she'd left her duties unattended. "She spoke well for Penwyck before the assembly."

Monteque's eyebrows rose fractionally. "I would expect no less from a royal offspring." He shifted a notepad on the immaculate desk, a subtle sign the discussion was coming to an end.

"When may we expect an audience with the king to discuss the possibilities?" Jean-Paul inquired, adopting the diplomatic "we" to remind Monteque he represented a country as powerful as Penwyck.

The hesitation was so slight as to be negligible, but Jean-Paul had been trained from birth to be aware of nuances. The admiral was uncertain about something and that something had to do with the king. Jean-Paul recalled that the queen had filled in for her husband at a state dinner earlier in the week. Hmm, interesting.

Monteque stood. "Sir Selywyn will advise you of the king's schedule."

Jean-Paul, too, rose. "Drogheda will not sit idly while weapons of mass destruction are brought into a neighboring kingdom."

Fury passed quickly over the admiral's face. "Surely Penwyck and Drogheda are long past those times when we tried to conquer each other," he said in amused contempt.

"A hundred years since our last conflict," Jean-Paul agreed, "but memories run deep. An alliance would go far toward erasing them."

"Perhaps Drogheda seeks more than a military and trade alliance," Monteque suggested, observing him with a speculative, almost hostile, stare.

Jean-Paul stiffened. "In what way?"

"I wouldn't advise one to toy with the royal princesses with an eye toward reaching the throne."

An urge to slam his fist into the admiral's impassive expression rushed over him. He managed a cool smile. "Excellent advice, Admiral," he agreed and, after executing a slight bow, left the office.

Outside, with the wind at his back and the sun on his face, he made his way to the royal palace, his fury unabated. Neither he nor his homeland came to Penwyck, hat in hand, seeking favors.

However, the situation with Megan complicated things, he had to admit. Her life and his own involved so many others. They had to think of the good of their two countries. To their respective rulers, no matter what the blood relation, the welfare of the nation had to come first.

A longing came over him, so acute it caused an ache inside his chest. His blood thrummed with the wildness of that night with Megan. He experienced again the untamed yearning he'd found in her...and himself.

But they couldn't be wild and impulsive. It wasn't allowed.

So what of that one night they'd spent together? another part of him asked just as furiously.

The arguments raged back and forth as he walked through the capital city. Pausing at one point, he gazed at the palace sitting on its knoll over the town and the sea.

He could sense the intrigue that surrounded the royal residence like a mist, gathering subtly and invisibly behind every corner, a threat to him and his.

A slight figure, hurrying from a large brick building, caught his attention. His body reacted, knowing her presence before his mind was sure.

"Megan," he called, and started forward at a run, then amended his behavior as several people stared at him. "Your Highness, a moment, please."

She stopped, glanced his way and hurried on.

Puzzled and irritated, he followed at her pace when he was no more than two yards behind. When she entered the public gardens around the palace, he stayed with her. At the family gate, she hesitated, then waited to admit him into the private area.

"What's wrong?" he asked, stepping past her into the rose garden.

Megan shook her head and made sure the gate had locked behind them. She went to her favorite alcove and sat on the wall overlooking the sea. Jean-Paul followed.

"Megan," he said more gently, "what has upset you?"

When she had the tears under control, she answered him. "I work as a volunteer at the children's hospital twice a week, or whenever I can." Her throat clogged and she shook her head helplessly.

"Yes?" he encouraged.

"One of the children…a little girl, only three…" Again she shook her head.

She saw he grasped the meaning of her despair. "Did she die?" he asked quietly.

"Yes. In my arms. She was an orphan, ill, and no one…no one wanted her—"

Megan stopped abruptly. Holding her breath, she sought the safety of her inner ice castle to contain the emotion, but Jean-Paul interrupted her efforts. He lifted her into his lap and held her close.

"I'm sorry," he said.

Such simple words, but they broke the icy control. She turned to him and pressed her face into his jacket. She didn't, couldn't, weep, but instead leaned against him, drawing from his strength as if immersed in a sea of tranquillity. He held her securely, not too tightly, but with a firm gentleness that soothed her heart.

The sun bathed them in dappled light under the birch tree. Bees droned happily around the flowers. The sea teased the shore with delicate kisses upon its cheek. The weariness of days filled with uncertainty and nights spent tossing in restless, impossible dreams overcame her. With him caressing her hair, she slept.

Jean-Paul leaned against a handy tree branch, testing it carefully to see if it could take their weight. It held steadfast, so he relaxed.

Gathering Megan's slight form closer into his arms, he looked out at the sea and the horizon so very far away. He'd wanted to sail to the world's farthest shores since his earliest memories, but he'd always gone alone in his imagination.

Brushing his chin over Megan's silky hair, he thought that sailing the oceans of life might be more enjoyable if one had a companion to share the adventure.

An odd thought, that.

Megan woke slowly, disoriented by the close beating of a heart against her ear. She lifted her head and stared at Jean-Paul. He opened his eyes and gave her a lazy smile.

She sat upright and looked around the leafy grotto. He half lay on the polished marble bench, his head on one arm, his legs dangling off the other. She was almost lying on top of him, her thighs across his, her head cradled on his chest, his arms holding her close while his hand idly stroked along her back.

Staring at his handsome countenance, she realized he was in the formal uniform of his country—white dress pants worn with boots, a blue tunic emblazoned with gold braid and a star-burst medal set with precious stones signifying his high position. He was a truly magnificent human specimen.

"I went to sleep. I'm sorry," she began in confusion.

"We all need a break once in a while, even a royal princess," he told her, his voice deeper than usual.

His hand slid beneath the sleeve of her knit summer top and caressed the bare skin of her shoulder. To her dismay, both breasts reacted, jutting visibly against the material in hard little points that begged for attention.

Lifting his other hand, he swept over them in a gentle foray, the smile changing subtly while his cool gaze grew warmer. She felt his passion rise, a hard rod against her thigh, and experienced an answer deep within her own body.

The wildness, like the call of the sea, stirred in her, that strange, aching desire for something more of life than what was offered. It ripped through her defenses and shredded her common sense.

His, too, she thought and watched in fascination as he turned them, pinning her against the back of the bench and sought her mouth.

"Kiss me," he demanded in a low growl. "I've waited too long for this."

She tried to shake her head, to deny the need, but his mouth was there, against hers, hot and firm and demanding.

The turmoil inside would not be confined. She kissed him back as if caught in the fury of a fierce storm, her mouth as greedy as his, her desire as great.

He cradled her head on his arm, their legs intertwined on the length of the bench. He pressed against her, seeking and finding a greater intimacy as their flesh melded instinctively, one made for the other.

"Ohh," she said as he moved against her, almost covering her now, his body stroking hers so that pleasure flowed from that point of contact to every tingling nerve.

"Sing for me, sweet selky," he murmured, his eyes hot on hers when he lifted his head slightly to gaze into her eyes.

There was something deep and mysterious and dangerous in those blue depths. It was like being adrift in a stormy sea, lost to everything but him and his touch.

Just where she wanted to be.

Closing her eyes, she writhed against him, drawing a gasp from his parted lips. He found her mouth again and delved deeply there, increasing the pounding of her blood until it echoed in her ears like the plangent sound of the sea far below them.

"You make me want to be wild," she told him, running her hands under his tunic and finding the silk shirt he wore. She tugged at the material.

He lifted his torso and sucked in his stomach so that the silk easily came free of his slacks.

"Heavenly," she said, "to touch you like this. Like that night—"

She stopped, not sure if she should bring up that memory. It seemed so impossibly long ago. Or like a dream that had never happened.

Only she had the developing child to prove it did.

Opening her eyes, she gazed at him, unsure of what they were doing, or why.

"It's okay," he whispered, bending to her, touching her with the sweetest kisses from his lips, so soft and tender and yet hungry and filled with desire.

Catching his head in her hands, she stared into his eyes. "How can it be?"

"We'll work it all out," he promised.

With a deft twist, he unfastened the row of tiny buttons that closed the front of her top so that he could push it aside. He stroked the satiny material of her bra before running the tips of his fingers over the burgeoning flesh. A half smile touched his mouth when he spied the closure. He unsnapped it.

A rush of fresh desire rose in her as the breeze caressed lightly over her breast. He kissed the tip before taking it into his mouth and circling it with his tongue.

Her breath caught, her chest lifted, and she pressed eagerly up to him, wanting more...all that he could give her...all that was hers to give him...

"Yes, come to me," he whispered hoarsely. "This is where you belong. With me."

His movements against her increased in a rhythmic fashion that fed the fire between them. Wantonly she pressed his thigh between hers and still wanted more.

"I need...I'm about to...Jean-Paul, please," she whispered back, desperate for his complete touch.

He kissed her in a hot, wild torrent of male need, all over her face and throat, murmuring lovely, wicked things as they sought satisfaction.

"Beautiful selky," he said. "My lovely sea wife. I didn't think you existed."

She rose to meet his downward thrust and wished the clothing that separated their bodies would disappear. She knew this interlude was foolish, dangerous even, but she wanted him...wanted him...

With a gasp, she realized he'd shifted again. His long powerful fingers slipped under her top and quickly unfastened the snap and zipper at her waist.

"We can't," she reminded him softly, desperately.

"Not everything," he agreed, "but this much..."

His voice trailed away into little kisses against her ear as his hand touched her intimately, finding the dew of passion she couldn't hide.

"Take all you want," he murmured urgently. "Take from me."

He absorbed the little cry she made when he rubbed sensuously against her and then deeply inside her, finding all the sensitive places of her body. She did the same for him, caressing the hard ridge with both hands until the world receded, drowned by the surging sea that lifted them higher and higher, then dumped them, gasping and stunned by the force, upon a distant shore.

"By the heavens, selky, but you come close to unmanning me," he said, collapsing against her, breathing hard.

Megan closed her eyes and wondered how, after

knowing him and this pleasure, she could ever return to her real life, the one that didn't include a rebel earl from another land.

"Princess Megan! Princess Megan! You must come. The queen wishes to see you."

The voice of her maid also seemed to come from some far place.

"We'll go together," Jean-Paul said, rising and helping her to her feet. He straightened his clothing while she did the same.

Before they left the leafy bower, he lifted her chin and looked into her eyes. "Aye," he whispered. "It must be marriage for us."

It must be marriage...

The words echoed through Megan's thoughts as she hurried to the queen's chambers. Lady Gwendolyn opened the door to her and dropped a tiny curtsy. "Megan, do come in. The queen is in her parlor—"

"Eating bread and honey?" Megan quipped as she and her siblings used to do, teasing their parents.

The lady-in-waiting grinned. "Yes. I suppose that means the king is in his counting house, counting out his money."

"See if there's a maid in the garden hanging out clothes," the queen joined in when they entered her sitting room, "and warn her to keep an eye on her nose."

Her mother looked at her own nose, which caused her eyes to cross. Megan laughed as she recalled days when nursery rhymes had filled the royal children's heads.

The queen nodded to Lady Gwendolyn, who closed the parlor door, leaving them alone. ''How are you feeling?''

Megan went to the window and looked toward the wall surrounding the palace. She could see the trees that shaded the alcove, but not the bench. ''Fine,'' she said, and felt self-conscious heat rise to her cheeks.

''No morning sickness?''

''No. Some. It isn't terribly bad.''

''That's good. Have you and Jean-Paul come to any agreement?''

Megan shook her head.

''Dearest, please sit down,'' the queen requested. ''I don't like speaking to your back.''

''I'm sorry.'' Megan sat on the Queen Anne sofa with its Chinese brocade print.

''You and he must come to terms soon,'' the queen continued. ''If word got out before your father is informed, he would not be pleased.''

''An understatement,'' Megan said, trying to smile but failing miserably.

''Well, he won't have you boiled in oil or beheaded,'' her mother assured her. ''He'll hold Jean-Paul responsible.''

''No, no,'' Megan protested. ''It wasn't his fault.

I was the one who followed him, who asked that he take me sailing that night. He didn't want me along, but then he relented.''

The queen's gaze shifted to the view of the sea outside the windows. Megan was silent as her mother looked pensive.

A soft knock at the door interrupted the moment. Lady Gwendolyn entered at the queen's call. ''The Earl of Silvershire,'' she announced. ''He insists upon seeing you.''

''Send him in.'' The queen rose. ''Jean-Paul, how lovely to see you.''

His glance swept the room, landing briefly on Megan before he went to the queen and bowed over her hand. ''Your Majesty,'' he murmured in his magical, lyrical voice.

Megan sighed, the weight of the past two months squarely on her shoulders. The price seemed high for one impulsive moment.

''You wished to see me?'' the queen prodded. ''Alone, or shall Megan stay?''

''It's for her that I came. I didn't want her facing parental wrath alone. Have you spoken to the king?''

Marissa frowned and shook her head. ''The king is extremely busy at present. It isn't the time for family affairs.'' She trailed her fingers over a large book lying on a table, then indicated the sofa next to Megan. ''Please be seated, and we'll discuss your situation.''

Megan grimaced at the word. *Situation.* It made the night seem less than magical, and that would be the way the press and the public would view it. "I don't think there's anything to discuss."

Jean-Paul laid an arm on the sofa behind her. "We must decide what is to be done."

"Jean-Paul is correct in this," her mother said gently.

"I won't be forced into marriage," Megan told them, sounding stubborn and childish. "Neither will I force anyone into it."

"If I had followed at once when you left Monte Carlo, would you feel differently?" Jean-Paul surprised her by asking, leaning close so that his scent enveloped her.

"But you didn't," she reminded him.

"I had several meetings already scheduled. I did send flowers. Did you get them?"

She nodded, unable to stop the furious blush that set her face afire.

The queen spoke up. "If you do not marry, then we must make other arrangements."

"My grandparents would love for Megan to come to them," Jean-Paul said. He smiled at Megan. "My grandmother will spoil you. She is mad for babies. My grandfather will start a cradle that will take years to finish."

Megan's mouth dropped open. "You have told them?"

"No, but I know them."

The affection in his voice touched Megan. Until she remembered that she'd had to send for him to impart her news. He hadn't come to her. There was no love between them, only passion. As those moments in the alcove proved.

"I would prefer marriage and the mantle of my name for my child," Jean-Paul continued. "For a royal such as yourself, it is the only way. Neither would I have my son's right to inherit questioned."

"You would want this child to be your heir?" the queen asked, her manner assessing as she studied him.

"Of course."

The queen smiled. Megan caught the glance that passed between the two, as if some accord had been reached.

"It may be a girl," she said, hoping it was.

He merely nodded. "Then my daughter would inherit. We must think of the good of the child." He looked directly at Megan.

Standing abruptly, she paced the perfectly appointed sitting room. "I think of nothing else. Concern for its welfare is with me day and night." She faced the window and watched a cargo ship push against the horizon, seemingly alone on the vast sea. The strangest feeling of loneliness washed over her. "If we marry, how long would it last?"

His quick footsteps warned her of his approach. Turning, she almost cringed in the face of his fury.

"No marriage," he said in a low rage, "has a

chance if you go into it with that attitude." He took a visible breath, released it.

She, too, sighed. Once she had dreamed of a storybook romance and marriage. Reality was very different.

"Fate has extracted a high price for one moment's folly," she murmured. Her foolishness had pulled him into the maelstrom, too. He had proved himself an honorable man, willing to take responsibility for what, in all honesty, had been her fault. "I'm sorry," she whispered. "Truly I am."

He changed in an instant from anger to that cool distance he maintained with the world. "Then you regret what happened?"

She could read nothing from his tone. "Yes. I never meant...it was only the one night I wanted..."

His gaze delved into hers, harsh and dangerous. "I see," he said, then spun and walked out.

The sudden silence after the slam of the parlor door hummed with strange portents, as if the gods smiled in wicked glee at the havoc they'd caused.

No, it was her own reckless action that had caused this mess. Megan pressed shaking fingers to her forehead. If only she could call back that night...

Her heart pounded in protest. If she'd never known the bliss of his arms, she would have gone through life vaguely longing for more but never realizing what it was. That night had given her a glimpse of what heaven could be.

If two people shared life as they shared their passion. If their dreams intertwined into one seamless whole. If they loved each other—

"Come," the queen said, placing an arm around Megan's shoulders. "You should rest before dinner, but first, there are things we need to discuss."

Seated on the sofa again, her mother beside her, Megan listened attentively, her own problems necessarily put aside in the face of duty.

"You must fill in for me on Monday at a street performance by the Theater Guild, then greet a group of American dignitaries, one of them a senator on a junket for his committee, and show them the palace. Gwendolyn said your schedule was clear."

"Yes, I was keeping my days relatively free in case the king called for my report on the trade conference."

The queen again looked thoughtful. "The king's time seems to be taken up with something…well, it must be important. I am filling in for him at a meeting with the Ministers of the Exchequer on Tuesday. You must attend, too, since you attended the trade conference."

"Does Father wish to press for ratification of the accord?"

"So Selywyn says." Her mother's smile was

rueful, but amused. "The king doesn't deign to speak with me on it."

"Nor me. He has never rescheduled our meeting for an in-depth discussion. In fact, I haven't seen him at all this past week."

Her mother glanced at a book lying on the sofa table. "I've spoken to him but once myself. Neither has he answered my invitation to dine privately in my chambers."

Here was a new worry to add to her own, Megan surmised. Were her parents not getting along? Her father had to put his duties first, of course, but he'd also taken time for his family, special moments when he'd suddenly appear, rush them all from the palace on a secret tryst to go swimming in the cove, or riding over the hills on the moor ponies, or simply to picnic under the oak trees in the garden.

She'd loved those moments with her family. They all had. It had made all the other responsibilities of being a royal bearable. She'd thought her own marriage would be like that. Duties, yes, but special moments, too.

A tender nostalgia rose in her. Those had been a child's dreams, based on a child's sense of reality. It had never been real.

Neither had the night with Jean-Paul. She'd been swept up in a great adventure, romantic and exciting…and as substantial as the selkies of folklore.

Laying a hand over her stomach, she knew it was time to put fantasy behind her and think only of the coming child. What dreams would the little one entertain? And what would be the reality he or she had to face?

Megan had no crystal ball to see into the future. Would a marriage between unwilling parents be best? She'd read that children paid little or no attention to strife between their parents as long as they felt, or assumed, the marriage was secure, but that divorce could be traumatic.

"Perhaps it's best not to bother the king at present," she said to her mother.

"Perhaps."

Megan summoned a confident smile. "I'll go nap now. Will I see you at dinner?"

Queen Marissa shook her head. "I have a state dinner. It's most inconvenient."

They laughed in mutual understanding at that. Their convenience was of no concern in the affairs of state.

And even less in the affairs of the heart, Megan decided later that night as she prepared for bed.

Chapter Six

After a quiet Sunday, Monday was the most hectic day of Megan's schedule. She attended a special performance of the Theater Guild in Sterling, the island's largest city, up the coast from Marlestone. Returning to the palace shortly after twelve, she hurried to the private dining room.

Laughter brought her to a halt on the threshold. Her two sisters were there, along with Amira and Jean-Paul.

The footman, also smiling, was serving the main course. "Your Royal Highness," he greeted her, setting down the silver serving tray and hurrying to hold her chair.

"Megan, do be seated," admonished Meredith,

taking the senior role. "We've had the soup, Cook's delicious minestrone. Shall we wait on the fish until you've finished the first course?"

"No, please don't." She smiled at the footman and avoided Jean-Paul's eyes. "I'll have the fish, too."

"Certainly, Your Royal Highness." As if he'd been expecting her to appear late, the footman set a plate at her place along with the others.

"So what did you think of him?" Anastasia demanded, returning to the topic of conversation.

"The stallion is intelligent. Also cunning. Watch that he doesn't take the bit from you," Jean-Paul advised.

"We went riding on the moors this morning," Amira told her, stating what was becoming obvious.

Megan had never felt so much the interloper as the earl and her sister and Amira discussed the merits of several horses in the royal stables. They disagreed on the abilities of the new stallion Anastasia had acquired, although Jean-Paul was impressed by the animal's bloodlines.

Listening to the debate, Megan realized that her younger sister was much more suited to Jean-Paul than she was. Anastasia was cheerfully holding her own in the argument over what made an excellent mount. Jean-Paul was quick-witted and animated as he gestured with his fork, driving home a point on the stallion's temperament.

Catching Meredith's gaze on her, Megan raised

her eyebrows in question, but her older sister merely shook her head slightly. Megan went on the alert. Meredith knew something the other sisters didn't.

A chill of foreboding seeped down Megan's backbone. She disliked secrets and intrigues and all the hoopla that attended life in a palace.

Life in a fishbowl, she corrected and had to smile at the hopeless fantasies that lived in her heart. It was time to get past those.

Slender but strong fingers touched her arm. "Won't you join us, Your Royal Highness?" Jean-Paul teased.

Gazing into his blue eyes, she saw lazy humor there and the smoldering embers of desire, carefully banked but ready to erupt at an instant's notice, given the time and the privacy needed. An answering flame leaped in her.

Why? Why did he want her this way?

"Of course," she said smoothly, keeping track of the topic under discussion as she'd learned she must do, no matter what other thoughts ran through her mind. Inattention was not tolerated in a royal.

"Perhaps you'll tell us of the alliance you seek with Penwyck?" Meredith suggested to their guest.

A pang hit Megan directly in the heart. Her quick glance at Jean-Paul caught the wariness that ran through his eyes before he smiled blandly.

"An alliance?" he questioned, an evasive tactic that Megan saw at once.

"Between Drogheda and Penwyck," Meredith continued, seemingly unaware of how her question affected him. "In a private communiqué from Prince Bernier, he asked that you be extended all courtesies due his emissary and said that you spoke for him. The king has asked me to represent Penwyck in discussions with you."

Megan gasped, then cleared her throat to conceal her shock. Jean-Paul was here for his country, not her!

She stared at her plate and envisioned herself locked in ice while flaming arrows struck all around her and fizzled out. Nothing could touch her, nothing.

Repeating that phrase, she listened to Jean-Paul's answer to Meredith.

"Penwyck sends their most formidable opponent," he said with a nod of respect toward Meredith. "I'd best be on my toes so I don't pledge Drogheda to Penwyck."

"What type of alliance?" Anastasia asked while Amira took in every word.

Megan saw intense interest in all three of the other girls' faces. This was sure to be talked about when they were alone, with much speculation on her relationship with Jean-Paul.

Her spirits did a nosedive. How foolish she'd been to imagine that he came only for her. He'd probably dreaded having to meet her face-to-face since he'd already guessed her news. If only she could turn back time and cancel that one foolish impulse.

"A military one, perhaps."

"Like that with Majorco?" she demanded.

He shrugged, giving away nothing. "An open trade agreement would also be useful to both countries."

Her younger sister gazed from him to Megan and back. An impish gleam appeared in her eyes. "As would a royal marriage, Jean-Paul of Silvershire?"

His laser stare subdued the irrepressible Anastasia. "My marriage…" He paused and cast Megan a level gaze. "My marriage will have nothing to do with international treaties or agreements. Not being a royal heir, I may marry where I please."

Meredith intervened, her voice cool, direct and protective of her younger siblings. "And does it please you to choose a Penwyck?"

"Perhaps," he at once replied, just as coolly. "We shall have to wait and see, won't we?"

The arch of his black eyebrows mocked the sisters as he lifted his wineglass to Meredith, then sipped the rich red liquid. Amira kept her thoughts to herself as she observed the play between the earl and the royals. Megan suspected the younger woman would report the conversation to her mother, who would then inform the queen.

Megan swallowed the last of the sherbet that had been served for the fourth course. She had eaten with difficulty, aware of Jean-Paul's dynamic presence at the table. Now she felt nauseated.

Rising, she said, "Excuse me. I have other duties." She left the room before the footman could open the door for her and rushed to her own quarters.

"I must rest a few minutes," she told Candy. "Are my clothes ready for the reception?"

"Yes, everything is as you planned."

The girl unfolded a silk chenille throw and laid it over her as Megan relaxed on the chaise in her bedroom.

"Leave me now," she ordered. "Come back in an hour to help me change."

"Yes, Highness." Candy disappeared like a shadow.

Megan sighed. She'd never spoken sharply to the maid. But then she'd never felt so upset. For several seconds she gave in to resentment and a bafflement of other emotions.

It did no good to rant over circumstances, she reminded herself sternly. Nor to feel jealousy.

There, she'd said the hateful word.

Closing her eyes, she sighed tiredly. She was jealous. Of Amira, who walked with the earl on the moors and entertained him with her knowledge of flowers. Of her own sister, Anastasia, who could hold her own in a discussion of good horseflesh. Of Meredith and her connections within the political framework of Penwyck.

Her older sister had questioned Jean-Paul in order to warn her that his intentions might not be so honorable as she'd thought. Megan pressed her fingertips to her forehead where a headache had started.

The almost silent opening and closing of the bedroom door alerted her to another's presence. She glared at her erstwhile lover.

"It isn't as you think," he said in his quiet, soothing voice.

She scoffed at the statement. "What do you know or care what I think?"

He stopped by the chaise and stared down at her, his eyes a mystery of shadows and thoughts she couldn't read. "I came because of you, because of the note you sent. Prince Bernier, learning of my trip, asked me to take over for his ambassador, who had taken ill suddenly. What could I say to my sovereign but that I'd be delighted to speak to King Morgan in his place?"

"Of course," she said coolly. "One can expect nothing less from a loyal subject."

He laughed softly and with irony. "I knew you would understand, Princess." Sitting on the side of the chaise and forcing her to move aside, he lifted a lock of her hair. "But my selky is angry with me. She's the one I hope to please."

Megan opened her eyes wide at the tender murmur, her heart melting at the tone as she studied him.

His gaze disclosed nothing but watchful wariness. She was reminded of how well she'd seen him play the diplomatic game during their week in Monte Carlo. Disgusted with her eager hopes, she put them aside and accepted the truth.

"Was the marriage bond a quicker way to an alliance, Jean-Paul Augustuve of Silvershire?" she asked boldly.

"I didn't plan that night, selky," he reminded her softly, still toying with her hair.

"You didn't send me away…after you had second thoughts."

"And realized the potential of such a union?" His tone scorned her argument. "A marriage of convenience has never interested me, Your Highness. But neither has leaving a trail of illegitimate offspring behind me."

His hand settled on her abdomen, sending shafts of warmth curling through her.

"Don't force my hand on this," he warned. "I can be ruthless."

"I don't doubt that," she told him, then was surprised at the retort and the fact that she felt no fear from his threat. She smiled, surprising him this time.

"You find this amusing?"

She nodded. "There is a certain irony. The rake ready to do the honorable, the maid refusing."

"Are you sure you're saying no?" He bent to her mouth, his eyes delving deeply into hers. "I could ply you with passion until your head spins, then you may change your mind about an alliance between us.''

She stiffened at his words. ''I will not be used for political reasons. Nor will my child.'' She laid a hand protectively over the babe, pushing his hand aside.

''Sometimes we are blown by winds we cannot change,'' he told her in prophetic tones, as if he brooded on some fact known only to himself. He grinned suddenly, which had the curious effect of making him look young and carefree. ''Sometimes the winds may even be fortuitous.''

He kissed her gently then, and she responded before she could stop herself. With a solemn gaze, he helped her to her feet.

''Come,'' he said, the mischievous grin still lingering on his mouth. ''I will escort you to your next appointment and show you what an excellent consort I will make. Candy,'' he called, giving her no time for reply. ''Help your mistress with her dress.'' He backed toward the door. ''Else I will be tempted to do so, and we may never make the meeting with the Americans.''

Flushed, Megan changed to fresh clothing and worried about seeing Jean-Paul again rather than what she should say to the American senator who wanted to discuss European trade and global warming.

* * *

Megan led her group to the palace steps. Standing on the topmost, she told them about the structure. "The main part of the palace, used for public functions and government business, was constructed four hundred years ago by Utherio, a powerful duke from a neighboring island."

"I thought a castle would have a moat and drawbridge," the senator's teenage daughter commented.

"It doesn't have battlements as he intended this only as a summer home. He'd conquered most of the tribal people, and with the fast sea currents here, he felt no need for more protection. Through treachery, his younger brother, Gunther, Earl of Penwyckshire, took the throne and finished the consolidation of the country, then named it Penwyck for himself. I dare not say more. Gunther was my ancestor…and his ghost is said to haunt the attics."

The group laughed appreciatively at the quip.

"Please come inside the main hall. Its size, large even by today's standards, was a marvel at the time. It's used as a ballroom on special occasions, such as a royal birthday or wedding, also for coronations and other matters of state."

Turning, she nearly stumbled as a wave of nausea rolled over her. A hand was there to steady her. "Thank you," she murmured to Jean-Paul, who'd insisted on staying by her side from the moment she'd greeted her country's guests at the town hall.

"You're welcome, Your Royal Highness."

He spoke the proper address loud enough for the Americans to hear. They called her "Princess" most of the time, as if she were a pet, but she didn't mind. They were candid and openly interested in her country and friendly in a natural, casual way. She liked that.

Standing in the middle of the reception-ballroom, she explained its construction and where each type of stone had been quarried and how it was transported.

"Let me show you the royal throne," she told them. "My brothers and sisters and I would take turns playing the king or queen and anointing the others as great knights. We gave quite stirring speeches on each other's valor and cunning."

The throne room was a small locked room near the king's audience chamber and contained only the massive throne of the realm. Decorated in purple velvet and inset with gold, silver and myriad precious gems, including diamonds that rivaled those of England's royal treasury, it was worth a king's ransom in treasure.

"The throne is moved into the main room on special occasions of state. It was last used to vest the twins, one of whom will inherit the throne, each as a Prince of the Realm, an official title. They, too, are addressed as 'Your Royal Highness' while the king and queen are spoken to as 'Your Majesty.' After my father's coronation, he mounted the three steps and took his rightful place as Morgan, King of Penwyck. At affairs of state, my mother occupies a smaller chair placed beside the throne. It's said Utherio had the throne built as a monument to himself, but only Gunther ever got to sit on it. So perhaps he was the rightful king, after all.'' She smiled wryly.

Megan answered more questions from the group, all of whom had become rather solemn as they gazed at the throne, which was, she had to admit, huge and impressive.

''The steps leading to the first floor, uh, the second floor,'' she corrected, recalling the Americans referred to the ground floor as the first one, ''have interesting stories—''

She broke off abruptly as nausea rushed over her again, causing a sheen of perspiration to break out over her entire body. Gritting her teeth, she led the way to the broad marble steps and ushered the group to the top.

''Here, Gunther—the kings often fought in their own battles in those days—defended his palace from invaders from Drogheda, a neighboring island country. It's said he slew fifty knights while standing right here, taking them on two at a time. A priest wrote the actual record, which was that he and two of his dukes did take on more than twenty-five foes, and destroyed them, thus saving the kingdom.'' She gestured toward Jean-Paul. ''The Earl of Silvershire reputedly led the Droghedans that day.''

Jean-Paul executed a perfect little bow in acknowledgment of her gibe. "*My* ancestor," he told the group with a charming smile. "We conquer by means other than force nowadays."

This last was said with a meaningful glance at her, delighting their tour group with the possibility of a romance. The teenager looked at Megan with envy evident in her heavily mascaraed eyes.

Megan managed a lame smile and continued with her duties. She still had afternoon tea to get through. "The offices of the Privy Council, elected advisors to the king, are up here. We also have one of the most modern security departments in the world."

As she turned to lead the way past the modern offices to a reception room where tea would be served, a sudden case of dizziness caused the palace to whirl. She held on to the railing to prevent a fall, then felt herself going over the balcony to the ballroom below.

Rough hands stopped the downward motion as her dress was grabbed and yanked backward. Then she was lifted off her feet and into a pair of strong arms.

"Take over," Jean-Paul said to the diplomat who accompanied them. "She'll be all right," he assured the concerned Americans. "Just too many activities and too much sun this morning. Excuse us."

He carried Megan to an elevator and whisked her to the basement of the building. There he hurried down the underground passage that led to the royal residence. In her chamber, he placed Megan on the bed and tossed the pillow aside so her head was flat.

"I'm okay," she protested, but her pulse was thready and her breathing shallow.

"Take deep breaths," he told her while he began on the long row of tiny buttons running the length of her dress.

"Your Highness!" Candy exclaimed, coming into the room and seeing them, shock on her face

"Get out," he said. "I'll handle this."

"But what has happened?" the maid asked, perplexed.

"She had a slight dizzy spell, no doubt from doing too many official duties today."

"I grew nauseated," Megan interjected, her voice stronger. "Perhaps it was the fish from lunch."

"Yes, most likely," he agreed to keep the young maid from leaping to conclusions. He had no idea if Megan confided in the girl, but doubted it. "Go," he told the dithering maid. "I'll take care of her. We have things to discuss. I wish her to plan a garden for me."

Wide-eyed, Candy nodded and flew from the room, probably to inform the other servants of this strange occurrence. Jean-Paul sighed gustily.

"We must put an end to this," he told Megan.

"Word is bound to get out. I'd prefer to talk to your father before that happens."

"Mmm," Megan said desperately, and clamped a hand over her mouth.

He looked around and spied a wastepaper can. Setting it beside the bed, he held her head while she endured a paroxysm of dry heaves. At last she lay back wearily, her eyes closed, her face pale as mare's milk.

"I'm sorry," he said quietly, guilt cutting all the way to his soul. "I should have been careful with you. I don't know what happened to my common sense."

"A strange, wild night," she murmured, as if that explained everything.

"Aye, wild it was, selky." He got a damp cloth from the bathroom, noting its precise neatness and lack of clutter. After sponging her face, he folded the cloth and laid it across her forehead and over her eyes. "Sleep. I think you need the rest."

"Who will awaken me with a magic kiss?"

His heart gave a hitch at the whimsical smile that tugged at the corners of her mouth. He suppressed the need to kiss her into wakefulness.

"I will," he vowed. "No other."

Pushing the washcloth aside and opening her eyes a sexy slit, she observed him for a long moment. Then she closed her eyes and, in a moment, slipped into sleep.

The turmoil he'd felt upon realizing she was

fainting stirred once more. He admitted the terror he'd experienced when she'd nearly pitched head-first over the balcony. Watching her sleep, other emotions roiled in him.

Tenderness, vast and perplexing because it made him feel unknown emotions someplace deep inside and he didn't know why. Need, its nature unknown to him because it wasn't physical, yet desire was part of it. And last was the hunger, part of the need, yet a separate thing, that made him want to sweep her up and ride off to a secret place in an enchanted forest, there to stay with her, make love with her...and to laugh and explore and delight in each other and their secret world.

It was damned odd, this mixture of joy and torture one slight female caused in him.

Love? Huh, it was nothing like the feelings that songs and poems led one to expect. Laying the damp cloth aside when she moved restlessly, Jean-Paul studied the face of the fair selky. He quite seriously thought she was beautiful with her candid green eyes and the auburn highlights in her hair hinting at fires kept mostly hidden.

But not from him.

Together they both exploded into passionate caresses and a hunger too raw to deny. Satisfaction spread through him as he recalled the desire neither could control. A most interesting creature, this sweet, elusive changeling who longed to return to the sea.

"But you shall not," he whispered. "You are mine now and must accept the fate the gods have in store for us."

He smiled wryly at the idea. Megan of Penwyck would obey no mere mortal. No, the fair selky must stay with him of her own free will. If she didn't choose to do so, then he would help her in whatever way he could, with whatever she wanted.

Stretching out beside her, he kicked off his shoes and cupped his body around hers. She shifted until she was snug against him. He sighed in relief. Her body knew, just as his did, that their fates were intertwined from here on out.

Queen Marissa paused on the threshold of her middle daughter's bedroom. Instead of one figure lying there, she saw two. Jean-Paul lay with an arm thrown protectively across Megan. A fluttery ache speared through the queen.

She was sure Megan was in love with the handsome earl. Even if she didn't admit it, the princess wasn't one to give herself lightly to a man. But what of him?

That he was honorable she had no doubt. That he intended to do the right thing by his child was evident. That he harbored some tender feelings for Megan was revealed in his protective manner. Was that enough?

It had to be. She had bad news.

"Wake up," she called softly as she approached

the sleeping couple. ''Megan, Jean-Paul, you must awake now.''

Jean-Paul sat up, the confusion leaving his face as he glanced at Megan, who still slept. He bowed formally to the queen. ''Your Majesty,'' he said.

''You must speak to the king at once,'' the queen informed him. ''I fear the news is out.''

''News?''

Marissa smiled in resignation. ''That one of the royal princesses expects a child. A London tabloid announced it today. Reporters are arriving with each plane and demanding an audience.''

''Do they know it's Megan?''

''Apparently not.''

''Then there is time.''

By now, Megan's eyes were open. ''Time for what?''

Jean-Paul touched her shoulder, so gently it almost brought tears to the queen's eyes. ''To face the music, Your Royal Highness,'' he said, a smile lighting his face.

A daredevil, Marissa thought as he helped her daughter to her feet. He defies the press or anyone to challenge him. Arrogant male. He thinks he can handle anything, but he has not seen the king's wrath.

''The king won't appreciate a scandal,'' she warned the couple, who cast each other a questioning glance.

"I won't allow Father to force a marriage," Megan stated.

Her daughter was showing signs of stubbornness that the queen hadn't realized the child possessed. And now was not the time for it, she feared.

"I have requested an audience. The king will meet with us in my chambers at five." Marissa glanced at the bedside clock. "That is less than an hour from now."

"We'll be ready," Jean-Paul assured her.

For a second, the queen saw a surprised but pleased gratitude dart over Megan's face, then it was gone. In its place was the composure of a woman who would not be coerced and the dignity of a royal princess trained from birth to handle any situation.

"You do not have to attend," Megan told him.

"Yes, I do." He gazed into her eyes for a moment, then turned to the queen. "We'll be ready," he repeated.

Megan hesitated, then nodded agreement.

Love and pride warred within Marissa's breast. She contented herself with a kiss on Megan's cheek. "I will stand by whatever you two decide."

Megan hugged her. "Thank you," she whispered.

Jean-Paul bowed crisply as she left them. "We must act," she heard him say as she closed the door behind her.

She wondered what her daughter would decide. Only the couple could work that out, but she did have some advice for the handsome young man who shared this conundrum.

Chapter Seven

Megan was ready when Jean-Paul knocked on her door at two minutes before five. She'd changed from her wrinkled clothing to a summer dinner dress of moss-green with a matching jacket that twinkled with sequins. Her escort wore a white jacket with a blue shirt and tie and dark pants.

Her heart started its acrobatic act.

"Beautiful, as usual," he murmured. He pinned a pink rose to her lapel, one that matched the rose on his.

"Old Pierre will set the hounds on you should he see you plucking his flowers."

"I stole them from the queen's bower."

He gave his wickedly charming grin that made

her want to run madly across the moors and leap from a cliff and fly with the wind like a fairy set free—

Behind her, the mantel clock struck five.

"We must go."

"Aye," he said, and tucked her hand into the crook of his arm. "Courage, comrade," he whispered.

Although she kept an outward composure, frantic thoughts ran through Megan's mind as they approached the queen's chambers. How could she explain a moment's rash madness to her father? What would he say...or do?

As they paused outside the queen's door, Jean-Paul squeezed her hand, then knocked. The door was opened at once by a footman. "Her Royal Highness, Princess Megan," he informed the queen. "The Earl of Silvershire."

"See them in."

The footman bowed the couple into the room. Megan's relief was short-lived when she didn't see her father.

"The king will be here shortly," Queen Marissa said. "Stay at the door," she told the footman.

"Your Majesty," the footman said, bowing deeply.

The king entered the queen's parlor. Pride filled Megan as she hastily studied her parent. He was splendid in a uniform of state, his figure still trim and manly, the white in his hair adding to his authority.

The queen rose. Together she and Megan executed perfect curtsies while Jean-Paul bowed. "Your Majesty," they murmured as one.

"Come, give me a kiss," the king commanded, opening his arms to the two women. He was smiling.

Megan kissed his cheek after her mother had done so. She realized he hadn't heard of the news in the tabloid and wasn't sure if that made the coming confession easier or not. A hand clasped her arm, warm and strong and supportive.

"Well, my queen, you called and I am at your disposal. Your wish is my command," he proclaimed effusively.

Megan wondered if the king, who had been rather solemn of late, had been imbibing too much from the royal cellars.

"Please be seated," Queen Marissa requested formally.

She served tea and small fruit tarts Megan knew her father was fond of. She relaxed somewhat. Her mother was preparing the way.

Glancing to her side after they were seated, she saw the amusement in Jean-Paul's eyes.

A vision came to her—of them in love, of his proposal being real. Then they lived happily ever after? Longing raced over her before she could control it, then she sighed quietly. She'd given up on foolish dreams long ago.

He touched her arm lightly, then withdrew his hand, a world of comfort in the simple gesture. It was odd, having someone at her side ready to come to her defense.

"To what do I owe the honor of this momentous occasion?" the king continued in a jovial manner underlined with a certain cynicism.

Megan studied her father, trying to ascertain his mood. She'd seen him but briefly during the past few months. He'd been serious, almost introspective, during that time.

Perhaps things were now going well with the country. The alliance with Majorco had been worked out. A public ceremony had been planned for the following month when the official signing would take place here at the palace.

"We have some news," her mother began. "That is, Jean-Paul and Megan have information you need to know."

"About the international trade conference?" King Morgan asked, his hazel eyes flicking over the couple, then returning to his queen.

"No," Jean-Paul said. "Our news is personal. While at the conference, Megan and I entered a liaison."

Megan would have laughed had the moment not been so serious. *Liaison* sounded official, as if planned, for something that had been impulsive and wild and so very, very wonderful.

The king looked confused. Megan knew the feeling.

"I am with child, Father," she announced stoically, and waited for his wrath.

There was a moment's silence, then the king laughed. And laughed. He laughed so hard he had to set his cup aside and cover his mouth with a napkin.

Megan felt Jean-Paul stiffen at her side. Her mother looked as astonished as she herself felt.

The queen drew herself up regally. "I don't see that it is a laughing matter," she said in a frigid voice. "The London tabloids have spread the word throughout the world. We asked your attendance so that we might form a plan."

The king underwent a transformation, the laughter abruptly disappearing. Now the expected anger surfaced. He perused Jean-Paul with open contempt. "What are your intentions, sir?"

"I have offered for her."

Again Megan discerned confusion in the king's manner, then he stiffened. "And?"

"She refuses," Jean-Paul finished.

Her father's gaze swung to her. "What?" he roared, rising to his feet. "What foolishness is this?"

Megan cast a frown at her lover. She would have

broken the news more diplomatically. "I will not have a...a marriage of convenience."

"Convenient or not," said the king, "it appears to me there must be a royal wedding. And soon."

"Your father is right in this," the queen agreed. "There is no need for scandal. Think of the child."

Megan nodded. "I am. I've seen the results of royal marriages beginning without love and ending in hate."

"There have also been failures that started out with a grand love proclaimed by all sides," Jean-Paul reminded her.

His tone made her feel childish for her insistence on a marriage based on something as elusive as love and mutual devotion between the couple.

"Yes," she agreed sadly. She dredged up a smile. "But I would have the illusion to begin with."

Jean-Paul became the distant, arrogant man she'd often met at public functions in the past. "You are a romantic. We must deal with reality."

"Yes," said the king coldly. "The reality is that we now face a scandal while we are in delicate negotiations with other nations. I have no time for foolishness. You will be married forthwith. How soon can it be arranged?

This last was asked of the queen. "A month, I suppose, would allow for the arrangements."

"No!" said Megan.

"Absolutely not!" Jean-Paul spoke at the same time.

"If it is against your wishes, you should have thought of that two months ago. Is that the correct time?" His eyes, flecks of brown mixed with the green, speared into Megan.

She nodded, then found her voice. "Yes."

The king raised his hand autocratically. "Then it is decided."

"We are not children to be ordered about," Jean-Paul informed her father, just as arrogant as the other man.

Megan groaned inwardly. If they would but shut up and pretend to agree, then later the queen could speak up for them to the king in a quieter moment.

"You dare gainsay me?" her father demanded, his face flushing with the full force of his fury.

"Not at all," Jean-Paul denied smoothly. "We must be practical. In this day and age, females don't feel the need of a man's name or his protection for their children. The princess is twenty-seven—with a mind of her own, I might add. She will not be coerced. Nor will I allow it."

Megan wanted to kick Jean-Paul to tell him to be silent. Queen Marissa, Megan noted, watched the king with her lovely blue eyes narrowed in thought. When she caught Megan's gaze, she smiled encouragingly.

Realizing nothing was to be gained by the meeting, Megan spoke up. "I will, of course, leave the country—"

"You will do your duty and marry," the king declared in frigid fury. "I order it!"

Silence followed this proclamation. Megan felt a cage close around her, trapping both her and Jean-Paul. A cage built by her own foolishness, she admitted. Remorse ate at her. She had also trapped the earl.

"Father—"

"We will speak more on this later," the queen interjected as Jean-Paul leaped to his feet and faced the king. "When we are calmer."

"I am quite calm," her husband informed her. "I have spoken all I intend to say on the subject."

"Of course," Marissa said calmly.

Megan knew her mother didn't mean it. She also knew this wasn't the time to pursue the topic. She, too, rose, and curtsied deeply to the king and queen. "By your leave," she murmured, requesting permission to depart.

The queen nodded. "You may go."

Megan grabbed Jean-Paul's hand and literally dragged him outside the queen's chambers with her. She didn't stop until they were safely in her sitting room, the door firmly closed behind them. She sighed as weariness replaced what little courage she'd had during the ordeal.

"My father is furious," she said, thinking over

the past minutes, which had only been twenty by the clock but felt closer to a lifetime.

"He laughed at first." Jean-Paul shrugged as if this strange behavior was normal.

"Yes, that was...unusual. I wonder if Father hasn't been working too hard. We've hardly spoken with him in ages, and he always used to make time for the family."

"Whatever the king's state of being, we must come to some decision about us. Do you wish the marriage?"

"I...not at the king's command."

Jean-Paul studied her for a tense moment, then frowned. His tone was impatient when he spoke. "Then what would persuade you?"

"Laughter," she promptly told him, a challenge in the toss of her head and jut of her chin.

"You are being frivolous," he reprimanded.

"No. I will not be pushed by my father nor by you into an ill-advised marriage. That path leads to disaster."

He moved closer. "How do you know?"

"Intuition, I suppose." She stepped back.

With a single stride, he placed his hands on either side of her, pinning her to the bedroom door. "It may be bliss. Perhaps you don't recall our private moments. Shall I remind you?"

His eyes issued a hot challenge. Something surged, wild and unhampered in her, struggling to answer. She fought the impulse until it was subdued.

"No, Jean-Paul, I have not forgotten," she said softly, "but we must not give in to that madness again."

"Sweet madness," he murmured.

He bent and kissed the side of her neck, sending tingles of electricity all over her skin. By dint of will, she remained still and unresponsive.

"What do you hope to gain by an alliance between us?" she asked, putting them firmly on diplomatic footing.

Tension invaded every line of his lithe, masculine body. Fury blazed in his eyes while his tone chilled her to the marrow. "You sell your charms short if you think I want you only for state purposes."

She laid her hands against his chest to hold him at bay. "I know you're concerned for the child," she began, then stopped as he slid a hand into her hair, freeing it from a golden clasp.

"There is that. And there is this."

Holding her captive with both hands, he took her mouth in a dazzling kiss that spoke of fires carefully controlled, of hunger that was insatiable.

"I don't like the position we find ourselves in any more than you, Princess, but it is one of our own making. I would pay the piper. Once married, we can do as we please."

A shudder of pain ripped through her. "I don't

think I am that modern-minded. I wouldn't pretend not to see if you entered another liaison," she said, using his word for their intimate interlude. "I wouldn't permit it."

A chuckle escaped him. "You sound like the king."

"Yes. We Penwycks are imperious and demanding."

"And fascinating," he added with a hint of other emotions besides amusement in his eyes. "Very, very fascinating."

When he kissed her, she didn't protest for a moment, then she shoved him aside, slipped into her bedroom and closed the door, leaning against it, her heart pounding.

After another few seconds, she heard his footsteps, then the closing of the outer door. The tension dissolved from her. Without ringing for the maid, she changed into a gown and robe, then ordered dinner brought to her quarters, too weary to face more of her family.

Think, she ordered after the meal, but she sat by the window, her mind lost in a mist of its own. When she spotted a lone male figure strolling the beach, she grasped the arms of the chair until common sense prevailed so that she didn't rush to him...

Jean-Paul spoke to Arnie Stanhope that evening. His friend was delighted with the burial chamber they'd found.

"Not one, but five chambers," Arnie exulted, "perhaps covering several hundred years, all with artifacts of daily life, plus—" here Arnie paused for dramatic effect "—totems and other evidence of a rich spiritual heritage."

"Sounds great," Jean-Paul said.

"It is. I thought of you every time we opened another section. You could feel the excitement with the first one, then the surprise when we found another chamber behind it. After that, it was just too awesome for words, and we worked in almost total silence on the last."

"Are you sure you've found them all?"

"Pretty much. The site appears to have been abandoned after the fifth chamber was sealed."

"Any trace of a village?"

"Not a bit. I suspect they brought their dead up to the mountains in a funeral ritual, but lived closer to shore."

"They were fishermen?"

"Yes. We've found hooks made from bones with every adult male and some of the females, even some of the older children, so it was a major occupation."

"What about farming?"

"We've found grains, but no instruments associated with farming, such as we know it."

"They may have simply used sticks the way the American Indians did."

"Yes. Uh, speaking of children—"

Jean-Paul sighed in resignation as his friend hesitated. "Yes? What have you heard?"

"This morning's tabloid said Princess Megan fainted yesterday and that she is, uh, expecting."

"Did it mention a possible father?" Jean-Paul asked dryly.

"Well, it said you caught her before she fell to her certain death on the ballroom floor below." Arnie paused again and cleared his throat. "The reporter seemed pretty sure that you were involved."

The slight question in Arnie's voice spoke volumes. If the article was definite enough to cause Arnie to question him, the report had been very convincing.

"Well, I suppose I'll have to confess all. Yes, the royal princess is expecting, and yes, I am the father."

A choking sound came from the other end of the line.

Jean-Paul had to chuckle at his friend's shock. As he'd often observed: Arnie was not of this world.

"I'd better call the parents as soon as we hang up," he continued, "else both will storm the palace here until they find out the truth."

"Your mother will be delighted at the prospect of a grandchild," Arnie said in his factual manner. "She has often said so over the past five years."

"I know. Keep me informed of the progress at the dig and on the artifacts. And the carbon dating."

"Will do," Arnie told him, then added, "And, uh, congratulations on the...uh...are you getting married?"

"I'll let you know as soon as I do," Jean-Paul promised. After hanging up, he sat in his chamber, deep in thought, then changed into hiking clothes. He needed to get away from the palace so he could think.

Crossing the family garden a couple of minutes later, he heard his name called. The queen was seated on a bench under a bower of roses. Dressed in white slacks and a silk shirt, with her dark hair and blue eyes, she was strikingly beautiful.

"Your Majesty," he intoned, and bowed before coming forward.

"Please, sit with me for a moment," she requested.

Jean-Paul joined her on the bench. The mountains along the coast, as well as the sea, seemed to stretch out before them into eternity. "I can see why you choose to sit here. It's lovely."

"It's one of my favorite places on the island," she said. "Just as the bench hidden by the birch trees has always been one of Megan's."

He hoped the heat he felt in his ears didn't mean he was blushing like a schoolboy in front of Megan's mother. "I know the one you speak of."

"Yes," the queen said.

The devil in him rose to the surface, daring anyone to challenge his right to know all there was to know about the elusive princess.

His selky.

The thought pleased him. No one else would associate the name with Megan, the Quiet One.

"I appreciate the way you've stood by Megan," Queen Marissa continued easily.

"I'm involved as much as she. More," he added in a softer tone, "for I knew where the pull of temptation could lead. She didn't."

"She's twenty-seven. A woman grown, at least in her eyes. To a mother, your child is always your child." She laughed quietly, but with an undertone of sadness.

Jean-Paul studied the queen. He put the question to her directly and simply. "What would you have me do, Majesty?"

"I have thought on it. You must woo her."

The surprise must have shown on his face.

She smiled, not without a certain amount of sympathy. "However you may feel, I think she would respond to a serious courtship. Megan, I am beginning to understand, has a bit of her father's stubbornness, but she is also tender at heart."

"Would you have me lie to her?"

"Would soft words and a caring manner be pretending?"

He considered, then said, "No. I do care about her and her welfare. As well as that of the child."

"Megan is vulnerable now. She doesn't want to force you into something she is sure will be against your will. If you want the child, you must convince the mother that the heart is involved." The queen sighed. "You young people are much more idealistic and demanding of fate than I was. I never expected love. Respect, yes. Kindness, yes. Passion…well, I wasn't sure about this last part, but yes, that came to my marriage as well."

"You're saying your marriage has worked out well?" he asked, not sure if this was true.

She plucked a rosebud and sniffed its fragrance, a sweet smile very like Megan's on her face. "It has. Sometimes you drift off course, but all will be well if you discuss the issues and what you need and expect from the union." She gave the rose to him. "Turn to each other with your problems, also with your triumphs. Share your feelings as well as your passion. There, that's enough. I'll say no more." She stood, indicating the session was over.

Jean-Paul kissed her hand and left her to stroll on the trail over the hills. Could he satisfy Megan's girlish fantasies by pretending to love her? The words were easy enough to say, although he'd never used them falsely.

In college, he'd thought he was in love, but somehow the feeling had faded. Contrary to that experience, he wanted Megan more as time passed, not less. And he did like her. She was smart, interested in all manner of things and fun to be with even without the passion part of it.

Heat gathered low in his body. But of course, there was the passion, a sweet, driving need that merely added spice to all the reasons they should marry.

Hmm, perhaps the queen was right. He would woo her and win her. Having made this decision, he felt lighter of spirit and turned back toward the palace.

A thundercloud rolled in, accompanying him on the return trip. He paused at the gate and observed the lightning play over the sea. Was the stormy weather an omen of things to come?

With a laugh that thumbed his nose at nature and whatever the Fates had in store, he continued through the garden.

The queen watched the storm approach and wondered if it was an omen of things to come.

Surely life was turbulent enough in the small kingdom without further strife. She sighed and wished for peace in her heart and in her family.

"My dear," a masculine voice said.

It was the king. Surprised, she stood and curtsied. "Morgan, how delightful to see you."

She wondered if that was true. Her smile wavered and disappeared as he came close.

"Please, be seated," he requested. "We have no need of formality between us, do we?"

A hint of wistful longing colored the question, causing her heart to contract. "Of course not."

Aware of his heat as he joined her on the bench, of the arm he rested casually behind her and of the sensuous smile that curved the corners of his mouth, she tried to figure out what was different about him…about them.

It was almost as if he courted her again.

An electric tingle charged through her nerves. It had been weeks since he'd been to her bed. She'd thought there must be another, but the way he looked at her now belied that idea.

"Do you seek me out to talk about Megan?" she asked, then went on quickly. "She was afraid you'd be angry."

"How else would I be?" he asked rather autocratically. "Has she no sense?" The question was rhetorical.

"Sometimes love happens like that." She heard the wistful need in her tone and hoped he didn't. His face hardened, so Marissa hastily took another path. "Yet you laughed when you first heard the news. Why was that?"

He hesitated, then smiled blandly. "Shock, I suppose. I came expecting a tryst with my wife, but ended up having to behave the outraged father. Did I play the part well?"

Whatever she'd expected, it wasn't this cool cynicism regarding their daughter. "Ah, perhaps too much so," she said, managing a tiny smile.

"What would you have me do?"

He leaned close so that she smelled the brandy on his breath. With one hand, he traced a line down her cheek to her lips and lingered at the corner of her mouth.

"Give them your blessing to do that which they think is best. They aren't children to be ordered about." She turned her head from his touch. "I think there is true feeling between them, but neither has realized it yet."

He frowned impatiently. "Then tell them they have my permission to carry on."

His harsh chuckle bothered Marissa. She studied her husband and noted again the almost feverish quality in his eyes. Worry ate at her. "You've been working too hard," she scolded gently, lifting her hand to his face.

Taking her wrist, he brought her fingers to his lips and kissed each one. "You're right," he agreed huskily. "Perhaps it's time for play..."

The electricity flowed through her again as his deep voice faded off suggestively. It suddenly angered her that he seemed so cavalier about their relationship, obviously expecting to be welcomed back with open arms when he'd hardly spoken to her in weeks and spared not a second for their family.

Pulling her hand from his grip, she stared out at the sea. "Sometimes I wish we could leave here and have a new life, one that's different," she murmured, an odd sadness tangling with other mixed emotions that she hadn't the energy to define.

"Leave?" He laughed as if this were a preposterous idea. "You would miss being queen."

"I would like a simpler life." She rose. "But as that is impossible, I must dress for the theater tonight. Do you join Gwendolyn and me?"

He looked regretful. "Nothing would please me better, my lovely queen, but I have other commitments."

She couldn't help it, but she wondered what they were. What had happened to the love she and Morgan had discovered early in their marriage? How did people grow apart?

Duty, she decided. They each had so many official responsibilities, not to mention those of family. She felt they had somehow failed their middle daughter. Megan, the Quiet One, the one who asked for so little, made so few demands, had always been easy to ignore because of her sweet nature. Megan, who at last had done something unexpected.

Gazing far out at sea, she understood what drove Jean-Paul to be something of a rebel. To be free, to roam the world and find adventure and excitement...

An idea came to her as she stared at the tiny

island in the bay. The storm was pushing the waves higher and higher. Soon it would cut the island retreat off from the mainland, isolating it until after the storm passed.

Which might be days.

Smiling with wicked intent, she hurried into the palace before the storm struck and lifted the telephone. "Selywyn, do you have a moment?" the queen asked.

"For you, my queen, I have all the time in the world," he replied gallantly.

"I have a favor to ask. This isn't official," she hastened to add.

"Anything," he said.

When they hung up, the royal secretary laughed softly, shook his head, laughed again, then went to a secure telephone and dialed a coded number.

"Yes?"

Selywyn explained what he wanted.

Silence answered him, then, "Now?" Logan asked.

"Yes. Don't forget food and bedding."

The king's top bodyguard gave a snort of laughter. "Are you sure this is part of our official duty?"

"The order comes from a high source," Selywyn assured his friend. "Be careful. The earl is strong and quite practiced in the martial arts, I understand."

"All will be as you wish," Logan replied dryly.

"Good. Call me when it's finished." Selywyn hung up, then picked up the palace phone and rang another number. "All is arranged."

"Thank you, Selywyn," the queen said softly. "You are a jewel."

After they said good-night, Selywyn stood in the dark of his silent chamber, his thoughts on affairs of the heart rather than affairs of state.

"Something must be done about the king," he at last murmured. "But not tonight," he assuaged his conscience.

Chapter Eight

"Where is he?" Megan asked, her glance flying around the hunting lodge built by her great-grandfather and remodeled by subsequent generations until, in addition to the huge log room, there was also a modern kitchen in one corner and bunk beds in a loft above the great room.

"You said Jean-Paul was here and needed me. Is this some kind of joke?"

Logan's smile was thin. "All I know is what I was told. I'm sure all will be clear soon." He straightened from where he peered outside the lodge window. "Ah, here they are."

Megan heard the *whomp-whomp* of an approaching helicopter. A minute later, a masculine voice she at once recognized, demanded, "Where is she?"

Jean-Paul appeared out of the storm, his tone worried.

"Here," Logan called into the growing dark, opening the door and walking out.

Megan stared in confusion as Jean-Paul appeared at the lodge door. "You're not ill," she said, beginning to feel like a fool.

"No," he agreed. An arrogant grin spread over his handsome face. "Why are we meeting like this?"

Megan strode forward. "Move," she snapped at him and pushed out the door. "Logan, come back here," she yelled at the royal bodyguard and his two minions, already in the helicopter, which had delivered her moments before Jean-Paul arrived.

Logan waved as he started to climb aboard. "Sorry, Your Royal Highness, but when duty demands, I but obey." His smile flashed in the growing darkness of the twilight and the storm.

Megan stared in disbelief as the machine lifted off and the three guards disappeared into the mist. "They've left."

"So it would seem."

She turned on her companion. "Did you plot this?"

"Are you out of your mind?" he asked equably, but hardly seemed interested in the answer. He flicked a switch. Lamps on tables at each end of a huge leather sofa came on. With that, he began exploring the lodge quite thoroughly.

Stepping inside and slamming the door when a gust of storm wind brought a heavy mist swirling about her, Megan studied Jean-Paul, who was on his haunches as he searched through a cabinet. She decided he was as innocent as she in this escapade.

With a sigh, she sank into a rocker set before the massive fireplace. Logs were already stacked for a fire.

"Who would have ordered us brought here?" she said.

"And in a storm. Ouch," he added, bumping his head on a cabinet door as he stood. He closed the door, then gazed at her as if worried.

"We're safe enough. The storm won't harm the lodge. It has stood on this mountain for over a hundred years."

Jean-Paul tapped the solid wall. "It's well constructed, but I don't relish spending the night. Do you know where we are and how to get back to the palace?"

She nodded. "But the path is too dangerous in the dark and with a storm nearly on us."

He looked her over lazily. "Then I suggest we settle in and play lord and lady of the manor. There seems to be enough food to get us through the next twenty-four hours." Bending, he examined a propane cooking stove.

"The storm may last for more than a day," she told him with a catch in her voice.

Giving her an enigmatic glance, he continued with his search. "Hmm," he murmured, standing on the stairs to the loft, eyes narrowed on the several bunk beds stacked along the walls. Under the stairs, he found the bathroom, which wasn't luxurious but contained all the necessities.

"This was built for all-male hunting parties, but my family started using it when Meredith and I were small."

"Huh," was all he said.

He unrolled sleeping bags, found two pillows, then blew up two air mattresses. In a few minutes, their beds were ready for the night. He'd put the covers on a lower bunk and the upper one that went with it. A shiver ran over her.

"Are you hungry?" he asked.

"No."

"I am." He opened a bag of cookies, ate two, then sipped from a carton of milk found in a well-stocked refrigerator. "Ah, all the comforts of home," he murmured with wicked amusement as he sat on a stool and leaned against the wall.

"This isn't funny," she informed him. "I can't imagine Duke Logan would do this on his own."

"I'd hardly think so," Jean-Paul agreed.

"The twins aren't here, so it couldn't be one of their pranks. Meredith and Anastasia wouldn't think of it. My father was furious with us, so I don't think..."

She was aware of Jean-Paul's light blue gaze on her as she ran through the list of possible culprits.

"So who does that leave?" he asked, a smile hovering at the corners of his mouth.

Dragging her gaze from his tempting lips, she folded her hands in her lap and, sounding as miserable as she felt, said, "My mother."

"Yes," he said simply.

Megan realized he'd come to this conclusion long before she had. "But...why?"

"To give us time to sort things through?"

"She's a romantic," Megan explained as if he'd taken offense at the queen's action.

"And you, fair selky? Are you a romantic, too?"

Meeting his gaze, she saw the fire he didn't bother to conceal. Wild thoughts of another night, another storm, raced through her mind. Longing gathered inside her like a collapsing sun, fiery hot and dangerous with the potential to burn them both to cinders.

She tried to suppress it, to ignore it when that proved impossible, but she was aware of Jean-Paul and their isolation with every fiber of her being. A slight tremor darted through her muscles, causing her to tense.

"Don't worry," he said in a husky near whisper. "All will be well. I can control my baser instincts."

"But can I?" she blurted, then flushed painfully as she realized exactly how she sounded.

Instead of laughing, his expression changed to one that she could only describe as incredibly gentle. "Tell me what you want, and that's the way it shall be."

She sighed, then smiled wearily. "I don't know what I want. I don't know what to do about our situation. I don't know what's best for anyone."

"We can discuss it in the morning," he said.

The mournful whistle of the wind increased as the storm swept over the sturdy lodge. Waves crashed against the rocky side of the island, visible from the windows along the western wall. Inside their snug haven, she and her guest sat in silence and listened to the tempest roar. Cold seeped slowly into the great room.

"Go to bed," he suggested softly when she shivered, then yawned and pulled her sweater tighter around her. "There's a pink fleece outfit in the duffel beside the door. I assume it's yours. There's a blue one for me."

She went into the bathroom and undressed, then pulled on the warm sweatsuit. After brushing her teeth and washing her face, she climbed the steps and crept into the lower bed. Jean-Paul stayed downstairs.

Her eyes grew heavy. After he turned out the lamps, she heard him come upstairs, then felt him step on her bed and settle into the top bunk. She

heard a faint thud just before he muttered a curse.
The rafters were close up there.

She smiled in the dark, feeling safe and content
for the moment. She would face tomorrow when
the sun came up.

The sky was still dark with storm clouds the next
morning. Megan was at once aware of where she
was. Looking over the rail, she spied Jean-Paul
standing at one of the front windows, his hands on
the sill to brace his weight as he watched the rain
pour down in heavy sheets.

Pushing the sleeping bag aside, she swung her
feet off the bed, slipped into loafers and went downstairs. A fire crackled in the massive hearth of the
great room.

"Good morning," he said. "Ready for breakfast?"

"Not quite." She stretched. "I'd like a shower
first."

"I found soap, shampoo and toothbrushes in our
supplies. Remind me to thank Logan for thinking
of everything."

She smiled at his wry tone as she headed for the
bathroom. As children, they had never noticed the
lack of amenities in the lodge, but now she was
aware that Jean-Paul had taken a shower before her.
She noted the razor on the sink, two toothbrushes
in the holder and caught the scent of soap and
shampoo. She hurried through her routine, donned

the pink sweats and returned to the main room as quickly as possible.

"Cold, huh?" he said when she paused beside a window and shivered as the chill penetrated the glass.

"Yes." She sniffed appreciatively.

He handed her a cup of coffee, then turned the bacon in the skillet. "Scrambled or fried eggs?"

"Scrambled."

"You got it. Sit."

She sat at the long table that could accommodate ten people easily. "Thanks," she mumbled when he gave her a plate filled with bacon, eggs and toast, a fork on the edge.

He gazed at her with a thoughtful frown, then poured a glass of milk and placed it beside her plate. "Eat. I'll join you in a minute."

As it had that morning on his sailboat, the atmosphere seemed intimate as they ate breakfast together. Each time she looked up, his eyes were on her.

"What?" she finally said. "Have I got egg on my chin?"

He shook his head. "Are you always quiet in the mornings?" he asked.

"I suppose," she began. "Well, I don't really know. I'm usually alone when I first wake up. That is..."

A grin broke over his face. "I understand," he murmured with a wicked light in his eyes.

He let her finish in peace, but he insisted on helping with their few dishes. She washed. He dried.

In ten minutes, they were done.

"Now what?" she said, not expecting an answer.

"Rummy. I found some cards. A warning, though. I'm a demon rummy player."

"So am I," she informed him.

"Let the games begin," he intoned as if they were the opening act of the International Olympics.

The morning passed quickly into afternoon. After lunch, they each found a book to read. Megan went to sleep on one end of the sofa.

Jean-Paul watched Megan sleep, looking pink and delectable in the fleecy suit. His body stirred. No surprise there. He tended to stay tense around her. The semi-erection went to a full one when she stretched like a cat awakening, then sat up.

"Still raining?" she asked.

"Yes."

"Are you grouchy?"

"No." He groaned internally when she struck a pose and studied him. By keeping a sports magazine over his lap, he managed to evade detection.

"Huh," was all she said, then she wandered about the room, peering out each window, until she came to the entertainment center.

"I've checked the TV," he told her. "All we get is static."

"We've never had good reception up here." She

stacked some records on a player. A pop tune with a lively beat filled the lodge. "Want to dance?"

"No." He regretted not putting on underwear upon rising that morning. "Excuse me."

Grabbing the duffel that had been prepared for him, he went into the bathroom, found briefs and put them on. With them and the navy sweats, he was decent once more. He returned to the great room.

Megan was moving about the wooden floor to the beat of the music. She changed steps frequently, obviously making them up as she danced. Her lithe form was sexy, all woman, although she didn't make any of those overtly suggestive movements frequently seen nowadays.

Desire increased to a maelstrom of hunger.

"Come on," she called, spotting him lurking in the shadows. She gestured with both hands.

Reluctantly he went to her. If she but knew where his thoughts dwelt, she'd hide in the bathroom and bolt the flimsy lock. Which wouldn't keep a determined flea out.

"This is good exercise and more fun than push-ups, huh?" she asked, her eyes alight with good humor.

"There's some that I like better," he told her, sounding like a disgruntled bear.

Taking one good look at him, she smothered a giggle, spun away, then spun back. He took both her hands and turned them in a disco move, shuffling her in and out of his arms, a matter of pure torture for him, but which she seemed to enjoy quite well.

He found he wanted to please her, that it was more important than his own bodily discomfort and general moodiness. Then he wondered about that.

"What?" she wanted to know when he grimaced at his odd musings.

"Nothing."

"You *are* a grouch."

But since she laughed as she said it, he was pretty sure there was no sympathy behind the words. He spun her around so that she was tucked under his arm and grinned wickedly. "Got you now," he murmured, and kissed her.

She went still beside him. Her chest lifted in rapid breaths, and he felt her swallow once before her lips trembled, then opened to his seeking.

He traced his tongue over her mouth, then dipped inside the sweet interior. His lungs stopped working properly.

"You really do take my breath away," he told her, grumpy again because of things he couldn't name or control and somehow feeling it was all her fault.

Which it was.

No other female that he'd ever met had confused the issues between man and woman as much as this one did. "I like things simple," he told her, glaring into her green-as-grass eyes, which seemed to hold laughter as she gazed up at him. He pulled her closer, wanting to feel the beat of life in her, to experience every breath she took...

He muttered an expletive. "What the hell is this?" he demanded huskily, at a loss to understand.

"What?"

"I asked first."

Her eyes grew rounder at his tone. "I don't know." Pulling away, she went to the kitchen and peered into the refrigerator. "There's chicken. Do you like it baked?"

"Yeah." Fists on hips, he watched her prepare their evening meal as if she knew her way around the kitchen. Soon, delicious odors were coming from the oven. Drawn like a moth, he went closer so he could observe her. "Where did a royal princess learn to cook?"

Megan grinned and wrinkled her nose at him. "When Meredith and I were little, we saw a movie where the family cooked a meal. We thought that looked like fun, so we nagged until Mother agreed that we should all make something. The palace chef nearly had a coronary when we invaded the kitchen and announced our intentions."

"What did you make?"

"Chocolate chip cookies, what else?"

Her laughter sent shafts of longing through him. "So when did you graduate to chicken?"

"When I was twelve, I started hanging around

the kitchen and watching the cooks. The head chef gave up shooing me out and started giving me chores.''

"Such as?"

"One always starts out on salads and cold dishes. Next I learned soups and stews, pastas, terrines and pâtés, then baked dishes and finally meats. Desserts, being the most delicate, are last.''

"A private education from a world-class chef,'' he said and thought of things he'd like to teach her. "You're a fast learner.''

"It isn't difficult when one is interested.''

Jean-Paul suppressed a groan at the images this remark conjured up. Like a dessert, she'd been the most delicate, the most inexperienced of his lovers. She'd also been a quick study, curious and intrigued by all that was happening between them. With her, lovemaking had been fresh and new and enchanting.

"Did you say something?''

"No,'' he growled.

After arranging canned pears in a baking dish, she sprinkled them with a cinnamon and sugar mixture and dotted butter on top. "Oh-oh,'' she said when she noticed a pot starting to boil. "Stick this in, will you?'' She pointed to the dish, then the oven.

Visions raced through his mind. Gritting his teeth, he stuck the pears in the oven with the chicken, which by now was smelling heavenly.

He'd never before realized that a baking chicken could be an aphrodisiac.

Or that preparing a meal with a woman could be so damn enticing. As she moved past him, he caught a whiff of the shampoo and soap they'd shared in the bath. But not at the same time.

That idea brought its own fantasies. He couldn't suppress the groan as hunger pangs of an erotic kind speared right down to the very middle of his libido.

Megan turned on him in concern. "Jean-Paul, what is it? Are you ill? That's the third time you've moaned." She laid a hand on his forehead. "You're flushed, too. I'll look in the bathroom for a thermometer."

He grabbed her hand. "No need," he growled. "You're the problem. The temptation," he added sotto voce and glared at her for putting him in this predicament.

Her alluring mouth dropped open as she stared up into his face. Understanding dawned. "Oh," she said.

"Yes, *oh*," he mocked.

Her beautiful throat worked as she swallowed. He took a deep breath and sought control of those baser instincts. It had never been this difficult in the past. Then he saw what was in her eyes.

"Megan," he whispered, drawing an agonized breath.

She turned from him. "Dinner is almost ready. There are some rolls to be browned."

He let her go, but he didn't care about rolls or dinner or anything but the woman who bustled about as if cooking were the most important task in the world. She removed the chicken and put the bread in to brown, her gaze carefully avoiding his.

The demon on his shoulder urged him to overcome her reticence. He could easily do it. She wanted him as much as he wanted her. He'd witnessed the hunger in her eyes and knew it was as strong as it was in him.

So why not take what they both wanted?

"It's ready," she announced, setting two plates on the counter. "Shall we prepare our plates and take them to the table? That seems simpler."

She wore no makeup at all, yet he'd never seen lips so pink and inviting. He took the platter she handed him and stood behind her while she fixed her meal. Realizing he was indeed hungry for food, too, he spooned out large servings of chicken and pasta and carrots.

"Wonderful," he said several minutes later. "Being abducted has its advantages. I'd never have known your cooking skills otherwise."

"Enjoy it while it lasts," she said wryly. "This doesn't happen often."

"Our lives are too busy for things other people take for granted," he commiserated.

She gazed out the window toward the rocky coast and the sea beyond. "Yes."

He heard the loneliness and saw the grief in her eyes for a second before she smiled, picked up their plates and began clearing the table. They washed up together.

The gray of the sky faded into blackness. The evening loomed before them. He brought in more wood from the covered porch and lit the fire. Soon the evening chill was chased from the room. He found that pacing brought no relief from the hunger that plagued him.

"Rummy?" she asked after he surfed the television channels and got only static.

"No."

She bent over a magazine and paid absolutely no attention to him. Finally she threw the magazine aside. "Will you stop pacing like a caged tiger?"

"I have to do something," he told her in a near snarl.

"We'll hike down the trail in the morning," she promised. "No matter what the weather."

"Fine."

Her face resembled a stone carving as she stared into the fire after their exchange.

"Hell," he said.

She didn't spare him a glance.

"Megan," he began, and didn't know what to say. He sighed. "I'm sorry. It's just that being here with you like this is difficult."

"You think it isn't for me? I'm embarrassed that my family put you through this. I apologize."

He shook his head. "That isn't the problem. It's me. It's being near you and trying not to touch you." He managed a smile and shrugged.

Slowly her gaze came up to his. Her chest moved as if her breath, too, was stuck in her throat. "We...we shouldn't."

"Why not? It's too late to worry about consequences." He grimaced at the cynical note.

She clenched her hands together in her lap. "I know. I wish I could take back that night. I wish I hadn't followed you to the marina. I'm terribly, terribly sorry."

If she'd kicked him in the solar plexus, he wouldn't have been more shocked. And angry. "So you do regret it," he said. "I'd wondered...but it doesn't matter. Whether you're sorry or not, the night did happen. We made love, and there's a child on the way. Live with it."

He walked out into the night, forgetting the pouring rain until the icy shower drenched him through and through.

It was what he needed, he decided savagely. Something to chill his blood and cool his brain so he could think straight. He stalked off along the ridge, stumbled over a boulder and caught himself in time.

Peering over the ledge, he realized he stood on a cliff that was at least a hundred feet higher than the gorge below where rainwater rushed with terrifying force on its way to the sea. Seated on the boulder, he thought about his life and the future. Usually sure of himself and where he was going, he discovered only uncertainty ahead.

"Jean-Paul," a voice called out of the blackness.

A light swept in an arc over the landscape. An ember brightened to a glow within. His selky had come searching for him. That had to mean something.

Chapter Nine

"You're soaked," Megan scolded, but not harshly. She touched Jean-Paul's arm as he entered the lodge. "And cold. Take a hot shower at once."

"Yes, Your Royal Highness," he said in mock obedience and kicked off his shoes, aligning them neatly on the natural stones that formed the entrance area.

Using a wad of paper towels, she mopped up after him, then added more logs to the fire. The night was turning really cold. At that moment, she heard the patter of hail on the roof and windows. There was no way they could leave in the morning. She wondered if she should mention this fact to Jean-Paul and decided he could figure it out for himself.

When he returned to the great room, he wore green sweats and thick socks. Settling on the opposite end of the sofa from her, he sighed gustily. "Ah, home and hearth. What more could a man ask for?"

"Probably a lot," she said ruefully. "One's own home or at least a hearth of one's choice, companions who are also friends."

"Aren't we friends?"

She glanced at him, then the fire. "I don't think so. You prefer those more like yourself, I think." She managed a smile as she envisioned the beautiful, competent women he usually squired about.

"You think I didn't notice you?" he asked.

She nodded, refusing to let the knowledge hurt.

"Then you're wrong." He turned and stretched his legs down the length of the sofa, enclosing her feet between his. "I remember you from Meredith's birthday ball. We walked together on the shore. You told me it was your favorite place, and that you liked being alone."

Megan tried to move her feet without his noticing. He clamped down harder so she couldn't.

"I don't think I'm going to let you go, selky," he murmured lazily, his gaze narrowed as he studied her. "I don't think I'm going to be able to."

His soft laughter confused and thrilled her. Breathing deeply, she tried to control the hunger that roamed her blood and lit fires at unexpected spots throughout her body. She almost moaned with the force of it.

"Do you want me half as much as I want you?" he continued in a thoughtful vein.

She glanced at him, startled.

"Ah, yes," he said in a near whisper.

The leaping flames became the most fascinating thing she'd ever seen. She kept her eyes on the fireplace as if her life depended on its heat.

"Would you have come out into the storm had I not returned to your light when I did?" he asked, running his foot along her thigh.

"You could have gotten lost. Or fallen. The ridge is considered dangerous for hikers in the best of weather."

"So it is," he agreed, his eyes never leaving her.

Clenching her hands together, she desperately tried to think of another topic. "I wonder who sold our news to the original tabloid who printed the first story."

"Your maid."

"I thought so, but the tabloid would have known it was me in that case."

"Unless she was scared to give a name that could be traced to her."

"The final story broke before she could have known, but it must have been someone in the palace who overheard us or my sisters and I discussing the problem."

He looked mildly surprised. "You've discussed the pregnancy with your sisters?"

"Not exactly, but Meredith knew something was going on between us. She, uh, arrived at some of the truth."

"You didn't simply deny everything?"

She met his gaze squarely. "No. I find it hard to outright lie, and Meredith knows me too well to believe a lie, anyway."

His feet continued with their wayward caresses as they speculated on the palace leaks. She couldn't summon the words or the will to stop him. As he'd noted, they were already paying the consequences of their foolish actions. Another night couldn't change the future.

Quickly, as if her longing might give her away, she rose from the sofa and stood in front of the fire.

Jean-Paul came to her. "What ails you, fair selky?"

"Us. Being alone. Everything," she confessed with a laugh that wouldn't fool anyone into thinking she was happy at the moment.

"I know," he whispered, moving closer. "It's confusing to be tugged one way by hunger, and another by common sense. I have a suggestion."

She looked questioningly at him.

"Let's pretend for tonight that there is no past or future to worry about, that no ties of blood or loyalty come between us, that you are not a royal and I am not of the peerage of another country."

"What would we be?"

"A man and a woman who have met and loved. Who are together after a long separation not of their choosing."

"A fairy tale." She clenched her hands on the mantel above the hearth and wished with all her heart it could be true.

"We can pretend that the only bonds that bind us are those that we choose, that we have chosen each other to love and that it will last for all time."

When she opened her mouth, he laid a finger over her lips and shook his head.

"For one night," he requested softly. "One night, selky. Will you not give me this before you return to the sea and your destiny there?"

She closed her eyes as pain rent her soul. "I want to," she admitted. "So very much."

"Then come. Take my hand."

Still she hesitated.

"Choose me," he urged softly. "Choose me, selky. As I do you."

Unable to resist no matter what sorrow the next day might bring, she slowly stretched out her hand. He didn't move. She laid her hand in his and swayed toward him as her legs suddenly grew weak.

He caught her to his chest. "You're mine now."

"For tonight."

His eyes glittered with a determined light. "Perhaps," was all he said, then he swept her up, took two steps and laid her on the sofa. ''Perhaps you'll want to stay,'' he said mysteriously as he bent to kiss her.

All else was drowned in the tumult of their kiss, and Megan forgot the enigmatic words.

She touched him desperately, wanting nothing between them. ''Take it off,'' she said impatiently and tugged at his sweatshirt.

He stripped it over his head and tossed it aside. His hands then slid under her top and pushed it out of the way. With quiet laughter, he nipped at her breasts until they were tighter than a new rosebud.

Tugging the fleecy garment over her head, she tossed it to the floor next to his, then ran her hands all over his powerful torso, loving the feel of his skin and bone and muscle, loving his touch, loving everything they did...loving...*him?*

Opening her eyes in alarm, she stared into eyes that were icy blue and hot with the flames of their mutual desire. His gaze trapped her, held her transfixed.

''If you're thinking of running, you'll not get away,'' he told her fiercely. ''Not tonight.''

''I couldn't go,'' she confessed. ''I want you too much.''

He watched her another moment, then he threw back his head and laughed. From that point, their lovemaking changed, becoming more playful but not less serious. She felt the passion in him, but also the absence of a tension that had been present.

Had he really thought she could go?

Sighing, she did as he bid and took everything he gave—and he was generous and considerate of her needs—and tried to give back all that he wanted from her.

When kisses were no longer enough, he rose and stripped the rest of their clothing away, built up the fire once more, then returned to her. Lying over her, his weight on his elbows, he instilled a sense of protection and caring in her that she'd never known with another, as if his spirit watched out after hers.

"It's odd," she murmured, laving kisses along his neck, "to find this…this fire…the wonder of it. It burns me to ashes, but doesn't hurt. Except for a little, deep inside somewhere. I can't explain…"

He caught her face between his strong, gentle hands. "I know, selky. I know this fire."

Content that he felt it, too, she gave herself to the hunger and the passion of the moment. The wildness of the storm couldn't penetrate the sweet cocoon of bliss that enveloped her or compete with the tempest that raged between them as he rose slightly, then joined them as one.

"So perfect," she said on a rapturous sigh. "How can it be so perfect?"

"Because," he said urgently. "Because it is."

For some reason, she understood completely.

Friday morning Megan woke in her lover's arms for the second time. They were on the sofa, a down comforter over them. The fire had burned to ashes and the lodge was cold.

Jean-Paul's eyes were open and on her when she lifted her head. Pushing her hair back, she smiled when he did.

"Did it snow last night?" he asked in amusement.

"It's cold for June," she agreed, shivering until he pulled the cover over her shoulder and tucked her against his side again.

He chuckled. "This weather would be cold for January, I think. Stay put."

She watched him rise and don the green sweatsuit before adding paper and kindling to the fireplace. The paper caught from the embers and soon a merry little flame was growing. He went outside and brought in an armload of wood, added it to the fire, then made three more trips to insure a good supply to heat the great room.

"I'll make breakfast," she volunteered.

"I will."

"You did it yesterday."

"Let the room warm up first then. I'll put on the coffee." He strode to the kitchen.

While he was busy, she made a dash for the bathroom. There, she decided to take a quick shower. Goose bumps appeared all over her as she undressed and stepped into the warm flow of water. Ahh, that felt better.

She'd just finished rinsing her hair when she

heard the door open and a cool breeze swirl through the steam.

"Mind if I join you?" Jean-Paul asked, then did so without waiting for a reply.

Before she hardly knew what was happening, his hands were on her waist and his lips had found hers. While he kissed her, he soaped his hands then rubbed them all over her back and down her hips.

Megan couldn't breathe as slowly he traveled up her sides to her armpits. He lifted his head and drew back slightly, his eyes dark and sexy as he covered her breasts and drew whirls of lather over each one.

After lathering her hands, she rubbed them over his chest and along his lean waist and down his hips to his thighs. She used the soap again and slowly gathered his erection into her hands and laved him there.

"Enough," he muttered after a few seconds.

Catching her hands, he brought them to his shoulders and held her close once more. Gently he washed her, then quickly washed himself. He dried them off on a huge bath towel, then used the blow dryer on her hair and his.

Finished, he handed her clean sweats, light blue in color, from her duffel, and slipped into the green ones he'd put on for only a few minutes the previous night.

"The coffee should be ready," he said huskily when they emerged from the steamy bathroom.

"There're frozen waffles in the freezer. How about some of those?"

She nodded, trying not to notice how he filled out the sweats. His quiet laughter brought her eyes to his.

"A man has a hard time concealing his needs," he admitted. "Women are able to be more discreet."

She put waffles into the toaster. "I thought, after last night, I mean…"

He poured them each a cup of coffee. "Once is not enough."

"Huh. What about twice?" she demanded, reminding him that the night had been deliciously long and ardent.

Cocking his head at a challenging angle, he said, "The third time should be the charm. Shall we find out?"

She held up both hands in defense. "Not until I've had breakfast."

His grin warmed her clear through. She'd never teased with a lover before, had never played these kinds of games. Love play was quite exciting, she found, in all its forms.

The waffles popped up. He buttered hers and his, then poured two glasses of milk. "Ready," he said.

They carried their plates to the sofa and sat on the hearth rug. He brought over maple syrup. Megan felt they dwelt inside a warm cocoon of enchantment as they ate in front of the friendly crackle of the fire.

The silence that lapsed between them didn't feel at all awkward, merely companionable, as if they'd done this often, as if they'd been lovers forever and were content in each other's company.

"It's nice—" She stopped, not sure he would share her sentiments.

"It is." He reached over and caressed her bottom lip, then sucked the drop of syrup off his thumb. "Just us, with the world far away so it can't intrude."

Happiness bubbled in her at the contentment in his eyes. She could grow used to this sweet intimacy with him. Fear darkened the bubble of joy.

"What makes you so thoughtful, fair selky?" he demanded, turning her face with a finger under her chin when she gazed into the fire. "I'm jealous," he continued softly. "I want all your thoughts this morning."

She summoned a smile. "I was thinking of you. Of us." But she wouldn't tell him of her suspected feelings nor the fears thus generated—that he didn't, couldn't, return those feelings.

Making love with her was a novelty to him, different because she was different from his usual lover, but newness wore off. What would take its place?

No answer came to her.

"You're sad," he said with unexpected insight.

"No. Not really," she amended when he raised a skeptical eyebrow. She sighed, already sensing the nostalgia of missing him when he was gone. "I was wondering if it's better to take what's before one, no matter the cost, or if, by rejecting bliss, one is able to avoid the loss and the pain that would come later."

"When the bliss is gone?"

"Yes."

Instead of laughing at her whimsical question, he appeared in deep thought. Finally he gave her a level glance. "I would never have given up our time together, even knowing I'd suffer hell forever after."

Her heart throbbed painfully. "But why?" she whispered.

He shrugged. "That's just the way it is."

Running his hand into her hair, he cupped her head and brought her mouth to his. The kiss was deep, exquisitely gentle and sweet. She closed her eyes and gave herself to the embrace, ignoring the odd desire to weep.

Falling in love was as new an experience for her as making love. Real or imagined, both played havoc with her emotions. Or perhaps it was carrying his child that did that.

"It's so confusing," she murmured when he released her mouth but continued to run his thumb along her jaw.

"What is?"

"This. Us." She gestured helplessly.

"Then we need to continue until we totally understand everything." His tone was mocking but his manner was moody, thoughtful and enigmatic.

She wanted to ask what things he thought they should comprehend, but he didn't give her time. Clearing a space around them and laying her on the down comforter, he made love to her again. It was as wild and magical as the night had been.

Jean-Paul watched Megan busy herself about the place. She washed his wet sweats from his sojourn in the storm last night, plus their other clothing and towels. He smiled as she became quite domesticated with a feather duster or vacuum cleaner in her hands.

But he knew her real nature. She was as untamed as the mythic selky he accused her of being.

Smiling, he waited until she'd folded the dried items—a washer and dryer had been hidden behind folding doors next to a linen closet—then he turned the tape player on. Soft music filled the room. He bowed to her and held out his arms in invitation.

Without hesitation, she walked into them.

They danced for an hour, moving slowly, sinuously to the music as if they were one. She followed his steps easily, something he recalled she'd done at her older sister's birthday ball.

Odd that he remembered so much about her and that night. Had it been an omen of things to come?

"You're smiling," she accused.

"I was thinking of the first time we danced."

"At Meredith's birthday ball."

"Ah, so you remember, too." That pleased him, but it also made him wonder at the nuances between them.

She stopped moving abruptly. "The sun," she said. "Look, the sun."

Going to the window, he stood behind her while the clouds parted and sunshine bathed the mountains in gold and caused sparkles to dance on the sea.

"The world looks new, all clean and fresh and lovely," she said, quiet happiness in her voice.

He looked at her beautiful face. "Yes," he agreed huskily and felt a heaviness inside. He knew what was coming.

In midafternoon, the familiar sound of an approaching helicopter confirmed his premonition. They were being rescued from their mountain aerie.

Duke Carson Logan didn't accompany his men this time. The captain saluted smartly when Jean-Paul went out to greet the officer. "Ready to return, sir?"

"Yes." He smiled grimly, knowing the queen would expect some resolution between him and her daughter. He would have to tell Her Royal Majesty that they hadn't gotten around to discussing the future. There had been too many other things claiming their attention.

His blood stirred lustily.

Shaking his head at this sign of unabated hunger, he went to collect Megan for their return to reality. "It's time," he said.

"I know." She hesitated, then gazed at him levelly. "Thank you for making things pleasant."

He questioned her with his eyes as he gathered the two duffels.

"Some men would have greatly resented being abducted and forced to endure hours trapped in a mountain lodge. It could have been very uncomfortable…"

Her voice trailed off as he smiled. "I can think of no better way to wait out a storm. I hope we can do it again."

He liked the pink that highlighted her cheeks and the way she returned his smile in her candid way. A treasure, his selky was, he decided. Their two days at the lodge had been very enjoyable, beyond any he'd ever known.

"Your Royal Highness," the captain said with a crisp bow to Megan when they went outside. He took the bags from Jean-Paul and stored them in the rear area while a soldier helped Megan aboard.

When they were all belted in, the chopper lifted above the peaks and turned south. In little more than thirty minutes, he and the royal princess were back at the palace.

"The queen wishes to see you," Candy reported as soon as they were in the family residence. She gave the couple a quick perusal, then stared at the floor.

"I'll change and go at once," Megan said. She paused at her door and looked at him.

"I'll go, too. Wait for me?" he asked.

She nodded, then disappeared inside her chambers.

Jean-Paul quickly changed to formal day wear, which was the diplomatic uniform of his country. Stopping by Megan's rooms, he found her ready in a day outfit of soft pink.

"You're more beautiful than a rose," he whispered before they reached the queen's door.

They were admitted at once by a maid, who quickly disappeared when they were inside the parlor. Tea was ready on a wheeled cart. Queen Marissa bustled in.

He bowed while Megan dropped into a curtsy.

"You're here. Good." The queen stripped formal gloves from her hands and tossed them on a table along with a hat that matched her royal blue shantung suit. "Megan, would you serve the tea while I wash up?"

She disappeared into the bedroom. Jean-Paul gave Megan a quick assessment as she took her place behind the tea cart. Her face was impassive, as if no emotion existed within her slight frame.

The Ice Princess was back.

He'd seen her adopt the mode each time she wanted to hide deep emotion. Only in his arms had he ever seen her drop the facade. A strange mingling of satisfaction and pride shuffled through him.

The door opened, and the queen returned. She was in an informal robe and slippers. "We have a state dinner tonight," she told them, settling on a settee. "I would like you two to attend."

He flicked a quick glance at Megan and caught the panic that riffled through her before she nodded. "Of course. What time shall we be ready?"

"Eight. The formal dining salon. Your father will be there."

Hmm, this could spell trouble, he thought and observed his sweet lover. She poured tea with hands that were as steady as a surgeon's. Pleased, he took the cup and presented it to the queen with a little flourish.

The queen gave him a smile of thanks and took a sip. "Perfect," she said.

He offered a plate of sandwiches and biscuits. She selected one of each and ate hungrily.

"Did you have lunch, Mother?" Megan asked with a note of concern.

"With the Privy Council," the queen replied, her delicate brows lifted in an ironic expression. "They have agreed to the Monaco trade accord on tariffs."

He noted that Megan seemed a bit uncomfortable. She was probably supposed to have attended the meeting with the council. However he felt no guilt about her missing the function. After all, the

182 THE PRINCESS IS PREGNANT!

queen had been the one to plan their little sojourn on the mountaintop.

Seeing the older woman's eyes on him, he knew he and Megan were expected to make an announcement. The queen would probably be furious when they told her there was no accord reached between them while they'd been secluded.

Secret pleasures stirred within him. With a stern admonition for his libido to be still, he wondered what Megan would say when questioned about the past forty-eight hours. What would he say?

The queen sighed, then seemed to notice them still standing. ''Be seated. You both look as if you intend to flee at any second.'' She smiled, but there was an impatience about her that he'd never noticed.

Her Royal Majesty was disturbed about something, and it was more than a wayward daughter and her lover or an international trade agreement.

Jean-Paul considered all the undercurrents he'd sensed since arriving in Penwyck, Thursday of last week. Today was Friday. Eight days. It seemed a lifetime, yet only an instant, as if he and Megan had stumbled into a time warp.

And only God knows where this one would spit them out.

At least monarchs didn't have one's head severed and stuck on a spike nowadays. He gave a sardonic smile at the image, then sobered as he studied Megan. She was coolly composed, ready to take whatever came.

Admiration grew in him. And worry. He didn't want her independent attitude to anger her father. She might not be locked in the dungeon, but she could be exiled for as long as the king chose, no matter what the queen might say.

Naturally he'd take her home with him, either to Drogheda or to his grandparents in France. His grandmother would welcome her with open arms, then pounce on him for not waiting until marriage to impregnate his lover.

Warmth crept over him. That was one thing he could offer Megan—his family's acceptance. They would love the child, no matter what they thought of the parents' behavior. He thought his mother would like the quiet princess once she got past Megan's natural reticence. No one could resist his mother's gaiety and gentle inquisition for long.

"Well," the queen finally said. "The storm has passed, and we must be about other matters. What decision did you two reach?"

Megan swallowed and looked toward him. Her smile, resigned to whatever fate awaited them, sent him an apology. She opened her mouth.

Before she could speak, he did. "We agree to the marriage, Your Majesty. As soon as can be arranged."

He could have heard a pin drop in the silence that ensued.

Chapter Ten

Megan returned to her quarters shortly after midnight. Jean-Paul walked by her side. The state dinner had taken forever due to the toasts by the Minister of the Exchequer on the international trade accord. She'd realized that Drogheda's balance of trade was much better than Penwyck's and wondered what they exported that other countries found so desirable.

She asked him.

"Fine craftsmanship," he promptly replied. "My grandfather noted that our people were skilled with their hands, whether knitting clothing or tying nets for fishing. He started looking for modern industry that could use those skills."

"What did he find?"

"Jewelry-making first, then carved architectural ornamentation. My father added labs for silicon growing and etching, also drug manufacturing."

She nodded. His information corresponded with the knowledge she'd gained at the trade conference and had been included in her report. Her own country exported a technical know-how in several fields, including medicine, science and engineering.

"Were you surprised when your father asked you to arrange a seminar on pathogenic neurology?"

"Somewhat. Meredith does most of the hostess duty in those types of things."

"And Anastasia does the sports events." His gaze skimmed over her face as if seeking information. "What is your specialty?"

"I don't have one," she admitted. "I fill in wherever my parents need me."

He frowned as if displeased. "That's one of the problems with being in our position. We must always do our duty, whether it fits with our plans or not."

She nodded, then opened her door and stood there awkwardly, not sure what was expected. "Should I invite you in?" she asked, stifling a yawn.

"No, selky. It's late, and you're tired. Rest tonight. We'll talk in the morning. Then I've got to call my parents, or else my mother will have my

head on a platter if our news leaks before I've informed her of our coming nuptials.''

"Our countries will have to negotiate the marriage contract,'' she reminded him.

For a second he looked angry again, then he
smiled in resignation. "I know. Let's keep it simple, huh?''

"Of course.''

Smiling at the absurdity of his wishful request,
he bent and kissed her, then shooed her inside.
"See that she isn't disturbed in the morning,'' he
told Candy, who rushed to the door when she spied
her mistress.

"Yes, sir,'' the maid said with a saucy grin.

However, Megan had hardly gotten into bed, the
light out and the maid dismissed, when the phone
rang. Her private number, she saw by the light on
the telephone. She answered.

"Megan,'' her brother said.

"Owen?''

"Yes. I, uh, heard some news today.''

She tensed when he paused. "From a tabloid?''

"Yes. Any truth in it?''

Huffing in exasperation at the speed with which
gossip traveled, she told him the truth.

"You're...expecting?'' He was clearly astonished.

"Yes, about nine weeks or so.''

"Jean-Paul Augustuve is the father?''

By his tone, Owen seemed to be having trouble

accepting her news. Megan knew the feeling. It still amazed her.

"What are your plans?" her brother demanded, sounding as autocratic as their father.

"Well, Jean-Paul told Mother we intend to marry as soon as possible."

Owen was silent, then asked, "And what do you want?"

It took her a moment to answer. "I don't know."

"Listen, Megan, the phone line is starting to cut in and out. We may have to hang up. Just promise me one thing?"

"Yes?"

"Follow your heart. Don't marry a man you don't love just because…well, because of one foolish night. You know Dylan and I will help you through this. So will Meredith and Anastasia. We just all need to stick together. Don't let Father force you into a loveless match that will make you miserable. Okay? Are you listening?"

"Yes. Thanks for your support," she said in a lighter tone and meant it. "Wherever you are."

She heard laughter in his voice when he answered. "I can't tell you where that is, but Admiral Monteque knows how to get hold of me. Call if you need anything. That's an order."

"Aye, aye, sir. Come home soon," she added, wishing he was there now.

When they hung up, she turned off the lamp again and sat there in the dark, thinking over their conversation. Owen was on secret military maneuvers somewhere in the world; Dylan was off on some mission. She had a sudden premonition that both of them should be here in Penwyck, that they were needed…

But no, that was just her own foolish desire for support, which she knew she would get from her siblings. She had her two sisters available, if she needed them. However, for some reason, she didn't feel like asking their opinion on what she should do.

Follow your heart, her brother had advised.

She wanted to. Oh, how she wanted to! Her marriage wouldn't be completely loveless, she'd wanted to tell Owen. Because with each day, she was falling more and more in love with her unfathomable lover.

Jean-Paul seemed set on the union, but why? Because he wanted the child? Because he knew of her reluctance and hated to be thwarted when he had decided it was for the best? She didn't know the answers.

Wearily she put the questions aside and forced herself to relax until she drifted into sleep. Her last thought was to wish he was beside her, holding her close to his warmth.

Nine o'clock had come and gone before Megan woke the next morning. Before dressing, she checked the weather. The day was overcast, but not cold. Out on the moors, she saw two horsemen racing across the rough grass that covered the hills and blew in the wind like a wave-tossed sea.

She saw Jean-Paul and Anastasia when they stopped at the stables outside the palace walls. Her heart gave a painful lurch. Given a choice, would he have chosen her for his life's companion?

That fanciful notion had been at the heart of her following him to his sailing yacht two months ago, she now realized. She'd fallen in love with him even then. That's what had gotten them in their present predicament. It was her fault. That much was clear.

Although he insisted on taking his share of the blame for their problem, someone had to be practical about their future. Sighing, she admitted that someone would have to be her. She would speak to her mother as soon as possible and get this straightened out. Then she would go away.

Choosing black slacks and a white cotton sweater, she added onyx earrings and a necklace for her morning ensemble. With sensible black flats, she felt capable and efficient as she looked over her schedule with its sparse assortment of official functions to be attended. If she pleaded fatigue due to pregnancy, she knew she would be excused from most of them, but that seemed cowardly.

Besides, she had new duties to attend to. Taking the stairs, she descended to the underground passage and headed for the infirmary and medical laboratory where important research was conducted. She needed to speak to Dr. Waltham, head of the medical facilities and royal physician to the Penwyck family.

"Hello," she said to the head nurse, who was studying a chart at her desk.

The nurse stuck the chart in a drawer, scrambled to her feet and curtsied. "Your Royal Highness," she said, looking upset and somewhat breathless.

Megan assumed she'd caught the woman reading while on the job. She smiled to put the nurse at ease. "I wondered if Dr. Waltham was available today. I know it's Saturday, but I thought he might have come in."

"Uh, yes. Yes, he is. I'll tell him you're here."

Megan watched the nurse flee down the hall and into the office at the end. She glanced around. The infirmary seemed unusually quiet. None of the royal family was ill, but the palace staff were also treated in the facility, as well as high-ranking officers and anyone with a disease that the medical researchers wanted to study. But that was done in an isolated wing so the contamination wouldn't spread.

"The doctor will see you," the nurse said, interrupting Megan's thoughts.

After discussing the seminar, which the doctor wanted to hold within the next week if possible, he added, "Only the one day. I already have commitments from some of my most prominent colleagues,'' he told her, and mentioned three impressive names in the field of neuromedicine.

She wrote the names down, discussed a few more and prepared to leave. However, looking into his kindly eyes, she felt the need to confide in this man who had delivered her twenty-seven years ago. There was nothing about her physically that he didn't already know.

"Dr. Waltham," she began, then didn't know how to continue.

"You know anything you tell me is confidential," he assured her, as if sensing her uncertainty. "Not even the king can make me disclose information about my patients."

She smiled in gratitude. "You may have heard the rumors about a royal princess being..." It was harder to say than she realized it would be.

"Pregnant? Yes. Is the princess you?"

She nodded. "I think so."

"Shall we give you a checkup and be sure?"

Thinking of the nurse, she hesitated.

"It will be totally private," he told her. "Come into my examining room."

He performed the exam in a matter-of-fact manner that helped put her at ease. When he finished, he confirmed her condition and advised her to take vitamin supplements and not to go horseback riding or boating or anything that could result in a sudden, hard jolt to the body.

"Otherwise, continue as usual," he said, "but don't overdo it on state affairs, such as the other day when you fainted."

"Oh, you heard about that," she said in surprise. "It was the sun, I think. I became nauseated. Jean-Paul saved me from a fall."

"Is he your young man?"

"I...he's the father."

The doctor patted her shoulder. "Your secrets are safe with me, young Megan, but they won't be secrets long," he warned. "Don't put off marriage. You and the baby will be better off having a settled life."

Nodding, she thanked the doctor and left the infirmary. Having official confirmation made the weight of impending motherhood settle heavily on her shoulders.

Laying a protective hand over the child, she knew they had to marry, but she was afraid. To end in hatred or indifference that which was begun in enchantment went against the grain.

However, there were acts and there were consequences. It was time to give up girlish dreams of a great and noble love. Reality was a marriage of convenience.

She smiled fatalistically. Or inconvenience, as the case may be. At least she was fairly sure that Jean-Paul didn't have another love he pined for. Maybe...just maybe it would all work out.

Thus speaks the optimist, she scolded her ever-hopeful heart, and laughed because else she might cry.

Returning to her quarters, she went past the king's chambers. Hearing a thump inside, she was surprised that her father was in his private rooms rather than the public ones he usually resided in during the day. She hesitated outside his door, then knocked softly.

Perhaps she shouldn't disturb him, but she wanted to speak to him privately about her wedding. A quiet one, without a lot of state pomp and ceremony.

Was that possible?

When she didn't get an answer, she knocked again, then, on an impulse she hadn't followed since she had been three or four years old, she entered the king's rooms without an invitation to do so.

The familiar furniture comforted her as she peered about. Closing the door swiftly behind her, she went toward the bedchamber. The hair rose on the back of her neck.

"Father?" she called.

No one answered. After calling again, she decided she'd been mistaken. He wasn't there.

The feeling that someone was hiding and watching her was simply the product of her unruly imagination, which seemed to have grown stronger as of late. However, she felt so uncomfortable, she decided to leave. At once.

Turning too fast, she grabbed a chair as dizziness washed over her. It was followed by nausea. She closed her eyes and held on until the spasm passed.

Feeling somewhat better, she opened her eyes. Before her was the pantry from which the king could have a snack whenever he wanted. Six exquisite little crystal jars caught a stray beam of sunlight and glittered like jewels in the dimness of the sitting room.

Seeing a tin of crackers, she peered inside and, noticing that it was nearly full, helped herself to two of them. The crackers would help settle the nausea. While nibbling on them, she examined the crystal jars.

Each held about four ounces of preserves. One had been opened. Lifting it, she unscrewed the golden lid, sniffed, then stuck her little finger into the dark purple jam for a taste.

Plum. Her father's favorite. Judging from the fancy containers, these must have come from a head of state as a gift for some occasion, perhaps his last birthday.

An idea came to her. The king loved scones, clotted cream and plum preserves. She would invite him to tea, then they could talk privately about the wedding and her wishes for a quiet family ceremony.

Yeah, right, some skeptical part of her mocked.

As if a royal could ever do anything as important as marriage in a quiet manner. She wondered if Jean-Paul had spoken to his parents yet.

Taking a pen and pad from a writing desk, she quickly wrote a note to her father and left it on the desk as she had done when she was little. Selywyn didn't like it when he was circumvented by the family, but sometimes subterfuge was necessary in order to get what one wanted.

She returned to her own quarters with a full jar of jewel-toned preserves. Suddenly starving, she opened her own private store, grabbed a cracker and wolfed it down. Calling for her maid, she sent the girl to the kitchen for a glass of milk and bowl of fruit.

After eating, she felt more capable of facing her duties. This morning, she would go to the children's hospital in town for two hours, then it was a luncheon with the Embroidery Guild. Hand-crafted lace was one of Penwyck's most delicate exports and in great demand by linen makers.

After lunch, she attended to the details of the seminar Dr. Waltham wanted Penwyck to host by composing a letter to each scientist. Once the formal invitations were printed, she reviewed them, then had Candy send them off.

Before lying down for a nap, she opened a package of Melba toast rounds and snacked on several. She'd been ravenous since rising that morning. Just another strange day in the life of a pregnant princess, she concluded and fell into a light sleep.

At four, she dressed in fresh clothing and called her father on his private line to see if he'd gotten her note. He answered the phone, surprising her.

"Yes, I will stop by, but only for a moment. I don't have time to join you for tea, but it sounds delightful," he told her.

She was pleased that he sounded so cheerful. He would be even more pleased at the news of the marriage. She hoped.

The phone rang. When she picked it up, she was informed by Selywyn that the king had to take an important call but would get back with her when he had a moment.

Megan thanked the royal secretary, then grimaced when she hung up. She'd really rather get the meeting over with. Spying the jar of preserves, she regretfully picked it up and hurried down the corridor to the king's chamber.

Slipping inside, she started to return it to the pantry and saw that the other five jars were gone. She looked on the shelves, but they were nowhere to be found. Had her father noticed the one missing and hidden the others, perhaps suspecting a servant of stealing it?

She sighed. She'd have to admit her crime since he didn't attend her tea. Feeling guilty for invading his private stores, she rushed back to her room, the crystal jar still in her hand. She would confess all when she saw him.

At loose ends, she wandered out to the garden. Usually she found her secluded spot soothing, but not today. She wanted the wedding ceremony discussed and arranged. Actually, she wished she could go to sleep and when she awoke, all would be over.

Then she would be a married woman.

A tremor rushed over her at the thought. There were so many questions, such as where they would live and what they would do to occupy their days.

Jean-Paul was trained in archaeology and went on digs with his friend, Dr. Stanhope. She'd read all about his interests in an article that described the earl as more than an international playboy. Would he want her with him if he joined his colleague on their latest find?

In some cases, the husband did his thing and the wife did hers and the two of them rarely met. Take the Duke and Duchess of York. Fergie had seen her husband a total of sixty days during one year of their early married life.

"Why so solemn?" a masculine voice inquired.

Megan stared at Jean-Paul as if he were a ghost. "Oh, it's you," she said, her thoughts in a muddle.

"Yes, the eager groom, rushing to his bride's side as soon as she appeared. Have you been avoiding me?"

"No. I went to the children's hospital, then I had a function—"

"Your maid told me," he interrupted her hurried explanation. His smile was easy as he looked her over. "Did you rest any?"

"This afternoon. I took a nap."

"Lucky you. I wish I could have been there."

A flush crept up her face. "I was hoping to speak to my father about...about the..."

"Wedding?"

She nodded.

"I talked to my parents yesterday." He held a birch branch aside and entered her favorite spot. Once he was seated on the wall, he took her hand. "My mother is too thrilled for words, according to her. Then she talked my ear off for another hour. She wants you to call her when you have a moment, if you will. She's in her office every morning by nine. I'm to give you the private number."

"That's kind of her," Megan said automatically while dreading the thought of talking to his mother.

"Father will have to speak to my uncle, Prince Bernier, about the marriage contract, then Drogheda's minister will speak to Penwyck's minister about the settlement. They will inform us what they have decided."

She heard the irony in his tone and saw the muscle tighten in his jaw as he recounted the protocol that would be followed. "You resent this," she began, then stopped.

His brief laughter was harsh. "I hate it that our private lives must be discussed and planned as if we had no say in it at all."

"That's why I wanted to talk to my father—to request a small ceremony with just family."

"That is impossible," Jean-Paul said grimly. "I am not so important, but you are a royal."

"Your every move is reported in all the major papers of the world," she reminded him.

He shrugged. "Gossip, mostly."

"It isn't known that you're the father. We could simply not admit anything. I could go away. It isn't too late. No one but our parents know of the wedding plans."

She envisioned the mountains and glaciers and that she was part of them, remote and unfeeling. Nothing could touch an ice princess.

Jean-Paul stroked her arm. "Come back," he demanded softly. "It is too late to withdraw."

She blinked as reality returned, its weight squarely on her shoulders. To her shock, tears filled her eyes. "I'm sorry," she managed to whisper.

"What's done is done."

She could read nothing from his expression or his tone. He seemed resigned to their fate, but it was clear he wasn't joyful over it. The guilt bore down more heavily on her.

Before she could weep all over him, she rushed from the alcove, across the garden and up to her room. Sending her maid away, she threw herself on her bed, but the tears didn't come. Instead they formed a hard, aching ball inside her that refused to dissolve.

She really wished that she could simply fade away like the morning mist on the sea. Then no one would be forced into anything because of her indiscretion.

Jean-Paul worried about Megan when she didn't appear at dinner. Only he, Meredith, Anastasia, Amira and her mother, Lady Gwendolyn, were present at the family table. The four women discussed their day while he brooded on his affairs.

The princess wasn't happy about their marriage. So? She should have thought of that before following him to his ship that night in Monte Carlo.

But she had joined him. There had followed a wondrous night of delight. Their time at the lodge had proved the night hadn't been a fluke. The second night together had been just as exciting.

So why was she reluctant to join with him in a legal ceremony that would please everyone involved, not to mention give their child the security of a father's name?

Was it a diplomatic problem? Did she know something about their two countries that he didn't?

"You're quiet, Jean-Paul," Meredith said, breaking into his useless musings. "Are you missing Megan?"

He glanced around the table, spotting the interest

in the women's eyes. They were sincerely concerned about him and Megan, he realized. His parents had been worried about the couple's happiness and well-being, too. He couldn't resent their concerned questioning for long.

"I'm worried about her," he told them, taking them into his confidence. "She's concerned with the idea of our marriage."

"I fear she thinks you will both come to regret it and perhaps hate each other," Anastasia said. "Megan is a dreamer, you know. She wants Prince Charming and all that."

"Yes, and you want his horse," Meredith interjected, frowning at her younger sibling. She studied Jean-Paul. "Have you told her you love her? Men tend to forget these things. They think women just *know*. Isn't that true, Lady Gwendolyn?" she appealed to the older woman.

"You may be right," the queen's lady-in-waiting agreed. "I should think an honest revelation of your feelings would be the most effective. If you care for her," she added.

The four women looked at him expectantly.

"Uh, I'm sure you're right," he said quickly. "I'll speak to her when we finish."

"Go now," Meredith encouraged. "She's in her chambers. Her maid said Megan had gone to bed with a headache."

After a second's indecision, Jean-Paul excused himself and went to the princess's quarters. No one greeted his knock on the outer door. He entered and went to the bedroom.

Seeing the door open, he went inside.

Moonlight slanted across the carpeted floor. On the bed, his princess slept with one arm resting under her breasts and one artfully laid beside her head on the pillow. She looked pale in the dim light.

A great tightening in his chest caused him to hesitate. He thought of the queen's advice to court his elusive selky and Lady Gwendolyn's to tell Megan of his feelings. He tried to determine what exactly he felt for this small female who had so forcibly caught his interest and imagination.

She made him dream of distant horizons and foreign seas and exotic things, he admitted. She stirred his body and filled his head with dizzy longing and emotions he couldn't define, ones he'd never felt before.

Was this love?

Shaking his head, he admitted he didn't know. He only knew he thought of her constantly, that he wanted to make love with her every night and being apart was torture.

Love? Maybe. Passion? Without a doubt.

"Move over, selky," he murmured, going to her bed. "I won't be denied this night. Whatever the morrow delivers, we'll face together."

Slipping his arms around her slender form, he cupped his body around hers and reveled in the feel and scent and wonder of her.

"Jean-Paul?" she questioned.

"None other," he told her, and kissed her delectable mouth. To his delight, she returned the kiss. He made love to her with all the gentleness that he knew how to bring to his touch, trying to tell her…to tell her…

No words came to mind, but he realized he didn't need any. She was all wild, sweet response in his arms. That had to foretell a fortuitous future.

Chapter Eleven

Megan woke to a muffled shriek. Startled out of a sound sleep, she bolted upright. Her maid, breakfast tray in hand, stood at the door, her face a comical mask of confusion, not to mention scandalized shock.

"Good morning, Candy," Jean-Paul said, also sitting up. He pushed a pillow up to the headboard and leaned against it. "Just leave the tray on the table. We'll serve ourselves."

"Yes, sir," the awestruck maid whispered as if her voice had been stolen by the sight of a man in her mistress's bed.

Which Megan considered perfectly understandable. She felt rather stricken herself.

The young maid left them. Jean-Paul prepared a cup of tea as she liked it, took a sip, pronounced it "perfect" and gave it to her.

He peeked under the food covers and found her usual fruit cup, whole-grain porridge, toast and jelly. He added brown sugar to the cereal and tasted, then added a bit more.

"Here," he said, and held the spoon to her lips.

She had perforce to take the bite. To her surprise, he helped himself to a spoonful, then gave her another. In this way, he shared the entire meal with her, a thing she'd never done before.

"An interesting way to start the day," he remarked when they'd finished every bite and were sharing another cup of tea. He gave her a sexy glance. "I can think of others."

"I have appointments this morning," she hastily told him, suddenly fearing that her father might appear with a royal brigade behind him to arrest Jean-Paul or perhaps throw both of them in the dungeon.

Jean-Paul nodded, regret in his eyes. "Duty calls."

Sighing, she pressed her temples and wished for a simpler life.

"Head hurting?"

"A little," she admitted.

He rubbed her temples for a moment, then gently pulled her into his arms, her head on his chest. "I think I could become used to connubial bliss," he murmured with a hint of laughter in his deepened tone.

Megan could, too. Too easily. She stroked over his chest and down his abdomen. He wore briefs. Recalling the night, she wondered when he'd donned them. Vaguely she remembered his helping her into her nightgown again before they settled into sleep, his arm under her head, his thigh over hers.

"I must stir," she said, but made no move to rise.

"I know." He kissed the crown of her head. "One, two, three," he counted, then threw the cover back.

Laughing, they rose—she to go to the shower, he to quickly dress. He was gone when she reappeared, but on her pillow was one perfect pink rosebud.

She pressed it under a tome entitled *A Comprehensive History of Penwyck: The Fifteenth Century*. Like Juliet, she wished for the soft trill of the nightingale, but the night was gone. It was time for the morning song of the lark.

Massaging the back of her neck, which seemed stiff this morning, she went to her sitting room and flipped on the computer. After checking the e-mail and answering several from friends who lived or visited in other parts of the world, she sat there thinking of the magic she found in Jean-Paul's arms. He seemed to find it, too.

Maybe marriage was the right thing for them.

Her feelings on the subject went up and down faster than a roller coaster, she realized. One simply had to take a mind-set and stick to it. Like a royal juggernaut, the wedding was already in the works. She should relax and go with the flow, as the saying went.

Except...

No! She wouldn't dwell on foolish dreams of a great love. With her eyes wide-open, she would accept her fate and be gracious about it. If it killed her.

With a fatalistic smile, she went about her royal duties, which were light that morning. First was another tour of the palace and Penwyck's ancient history for foreign visitors, then luncheon, this time a fund-raiser for the children's hospital, her favorite charity.

By three, she had returned to her quarters, the headache more fierce than ever. An odd chill caused her to shiver as she reclined on the chaise lounge. She pulled the finely woven afghan over her and sank instantly into sleep.

Jean-Paul stood at the window of his bedroom and watched the gardens below. He was restless, and he knew the cause. He was impatient to see Megan.

The maid had informed him that Her Royal Highness was sleeping. He hadn't the heart to disturb her. Perhaps it was the pregnancy, but Megan seemed tired of late and vulnerable in a way he hadn't been aware of in their past dealings.

In truth, he was worried about her. All this stress couldn't be good for her or the baby.

His insides tightened convulsively at the thought of the child. His. And hers. A life created out of their passionate interlude. A symbol of the future, of hope and happiness to come.

He shook his head at the odd musings. Of late, he thought more and more of the future and his role as a husband and father. Although the rebel in him decried a forced marriage, another part embraced the idea.

And that was the oddest thing of all.

Just as he started to turn away, he spotted movement in the garden. The queen walked alone among the roses, stopping every few feet to sniff a blossom or remove a faded one from the vine. He wondered at her relationship with the king.

In truth, he'd never seen them together in the private family quarters and only once or twice at the state functions he'd attended as emissary from his country. He'd had a lengthy conversation with his uncle, Prince Bernier, that morning on a code-scrambled cell phone. The prince adamantly wanted to be part of any military alliance between the island kingdoms.

Easier said than done, Jean-Paul had felt like telling the prince. Naturally, he'd guarded his tongue.

The queen suddenly stopped, her entire posture

going stiff with surprise, then she relaxed. Jean-Paul saw her nod, then he spied the king. Morgan joined his queen, holding out an arm to her in a gallant fashion.

They strolled among the roses for perhaps ten minutes, chatting amiably, if one could go by their manner and gestures. King Morgan stopped beside a rosebush and plucked a white rose whose petals were edged in a pink blush. He removed the thorns from its stem.

To Jean-Paul's amusement, the king touched his lips to the rose, then brushed it along the queen's cheek to her mouth, lingered there a second, then dipped to a point between her breasts. In a loverlike manner, he slipped the rose into the queen's cleavage. They stood very close.

Hmm, it would appear the couple was much closer than gossip indicated these days.

The king bent his head toward the queen, obviously intending to kiss her. Jean-Paul, feeling intrusive, decided to withdraw, but at that moment, another figure appeared.

The king stepped away from the queen, who pressed a hand to her breast as if flustered. Jean-Paul saw the other man was Duke Carson Logan, the royal bodyguard. He spoke to the king for a moment. The king nodded, then kissed the queen's hand.

When the men were gone, the queen took a seat

in her favorite rose bower, her movements pensive, perhaps sad.

Jean-Paul wondered how anyone in public life ever had a private one. A rueful smile curved his mouth. Morgan and his queen had produced three girls and twin boys, so they must have had some quiet moments.

Recalling his own trysts with Megan, he turned from the window. His mother, aware that the wedding must be rushed, was determined to speak to the bride-to-be as soon as possible. He was to deliver a message to Megan to call at once. Suppressing the throb of hunger he felt each time he thought of the princess, he hurried to her chamber to see if she was awake.

The young maid greeted him with the news that the princess was still sleeping.

"I need to talk to her," he said, frowning at the delay. "Awaken her."

"Oh, sir, I cannot. The queen said the princess wasn't to be disturbed."

"The queen was here? When?"

"About an hour ago." The girl was obviously worried out of her wits about something.

"What ails you?" he asked on a kinder note.

Candy caught her lower lip between her teeth. She glanced over her shoulder. Following her gaze, Jean-Paul went to the writing desk. A tabloid was placed there, its pages folded to a headline.

"Royal Princess Pregnant by Playboy Earl," he

read. He cursed softly. A picture of him and Megan coming out of the conference room in Monte Carlo—they happened to be leaving at the same moment, but not together—was prominently displayed under the inch-high letters.

The tabloid seemed to have all the details, except the reporters hadn't known about Megan being on his ship.

However, they did have the dates and length of her pregnancy correct. Putting two and two together with his being in Penwyck and staying in the royal residence, they had concluded that he was the father and that an official wedding would soon be announced. There was the usual speculation on their being in love and whether their parents approved of the match.

He groaned and cursed again.

Megan would be mortified and even more reluctant to wed under the circumstances. At that moment, she appeared in the bedroom doorway, looking lovely and flushed and heavy eyed, as if they'd just made love.

His blood warmed at the sight, and he went to her, drawn as surely as the proverbial moth to flame.

As soon as he touched her, though, he went from hunger to worry. "You're hot," he said, puzzled.

She giggled. "We used to play 'find the thimble' when we were little. We gave each other clues—

you're hot or you're cold, according to whether we were close to the hiding place or not.''

He ignored her rambling talk and laid a hand on her forehead. She was burning up, her skin dry and hot with fever. Fear darted through him.

''Come on,'' he told her, taking her hand.

She followed him willingly. ''Where are we going?''

''To the infirmary.''

''I've already seen Dr. Waltham. He confirmed our news.'' She glanced at her maid, who watched with wide eyes, then covered her mouth as if to hold in their secret.

''All the world knows,'' he said, leading her down the corridor to the stairs.

''What?''

''That you're pregnant and I'm the father.''

''Oh.'' A sorrowful expression turned her mouth down. ''I'm terribly sorry, Jean-Paul, for getting you into this.''

''Just shut up,'' he ordered, rushing her down the stone steps to the underground passageways.

She sniffed like a child trying not to cry.

His concern grew. ''Where's Dr. Waltham?'' he asked the nurse at the infirmary desk.

The woman glanced toward an office. Jean-Paul didn't wait, but went at once to the room. An older man with white, wiry hair and eyebrows glanced up at him, surprise on his lined face. The doctor laid aside the paper he was reading.

"Megan's ill," Jean-Paul announced.

Alarm flashed through the doctor's dark eyes. "In here," he ordered, and led the way to a medical examination room. "When did she take sick?"

"After lunch, I think," Jean-Paul reported. "She was sleeping. I needed to see her. She felt hot."

The doctor nodded, as if the succinct explanation made sense, and had Megan sit on the table. He stuck a thermometer in her ear, then let out a hissing breath.

"You're right. She's burning up." He went to the door. "Nurse Dora, I need your help."

The nurse came at once. "Yes, Doctor?"

Jean-Paul noted the exchange of glances between the two. The hair stood up on the back of his neck. "What is it? What does she have?" he demanded.

"I don't know. We'll have to check. The works," the doctor said to the nurse. "Full blood tests. Tell the lab I want the results today. Make that clear."

"Yes, sir." The nurse bustled around in an efficient, nonhurried manner that got things done.

"I'm giving her a fever reducer," Dr. Waltham told Jean-Paul as he stuck a needle into Megan's arm.

"Ouch," she said, and frowned at them. After covering a yawn, she told them she wanted to go back to bed.

"Good idea," Waltham agreed. "The isolation ward," he told the nurse. "Room two."

"Right. I'll get a wheelchair."

"I can walk," Megan said indignantly.

"Hush," Jean-Paul ordered. "You'll do as told."

Worry gnawed at him like a pack of wharf rats. He sensed the seriousness of the situation and all that the doctor didn't say. "Why isolation?" he asked, helping Megan into the wheelchair the nurse brought.

The doctor hesitated, then shrugged. "She may have something contagious."

"She volunteers at the children's hospital in town," Jean-Paul told him. "Last week a child died in her arms."

"Hmm," was all the doctor said.

The doctor didn't seem concerned about the connection to the child at all. Jean-Paul set his teeth together to keep from cursing the medical team as they took Megan to another wing of the infirmary and, telling him to wait, disappeared from view.

He paced the floor, a thing he'd never done in his life. An hour passed before the nurse returned to the nursing station.

"Well?" he asked impatiently. "How is she?"

"Resting."

"What's wrong with her?"

"You'll have to ask the doctor."

He took a deep breath. "All right. Where is he?"

"Dr. Waltham is busy. He can't see you now."

"When will he be available?"

"I don't know."

Jean-Paul considered leaping over the counter and strangling the woman. With superhuman effort, he refrained. "Fine," he said, his jaw so tight he could hardly speak. "I'll wait in his office."

That got her attention. "You can't do that!"

"Watch me," he said in a snarl. He marched into the doctor's office, straddled a chair and waited.

And waited.

The traffic in and out of the isolation ward increased steadily as medical technicians, nurses and some others whose function wasn't clear to him came and went with great regularity. Dr. Waltham didn't reappear.

At seven, the queen appeared. She rushed into the office looking as grim and worried as he felt.

"Where's the doctor?" she demanded.

"Beats me," Jean-Paul admitted. "He took Megan into the isolation ward and never returned. Did they tell you anything about her?"

"No."

"Me, either." He glared at the swinging door as another cadre of medical people went through. "Wait here."

He went into the quarantined area, determined to find Waltham and demand to know what was wrong.

"Sir, you're not allowed in here! This is the isolation ward," a young male nurse told him and pointed back toward the doors. "Please leave at once."

Jean-Paul took a fighting stance. "Not until I get some answers. Where's the damn doctor?"

"Here," Dr. Waltham spoke up, coming out of a room and closing the door behind him.

Jean-Paul noted it was numbered with a one on the door. He glanced across the corridor to the door marked with a two. Were there two patients in the ward?

"The queen is in your office," he told the man. "We want to know about Megan."

Again Jean-Paul caught the look that passed between the doctor and the other medical person.

"I'll be back shortly," Waltham said to the nurse, then led the way to his office. "Your Majesty," he murmured to the queen, and gave a slight bow.

She nodded regally, looking every inch a queen. "What's wrong with my daughter?"

"Please, be seated," the doctor offered, glancing from one to the other.

Jean-Paul seated the queen, then took the other chair.

"The princess has a fever, also aches and chills similar to the influenza," Waltham told them.

"Is it the flu?" Jean-Paul demanded.

"I...uh, no, I don't think so."

"Then what?" Queen Marissa asked.

The doctor sighed wearily. "Frankly, I'm not sure. We're running lab tests. As soon as we get the results, I'll let you know."

This last was said to the queen, clearly leaving Jean-Paul out of the loop. He realized he couldn't claim a husband's privileges and demand to be kept informed.

The queen stood. "All right. I want to be informed if there's any change, for better or worse. Is that clear?"

The doctor, leaping to his feet, nodded formally. "Yes, Majesty, of course."

"The earl and the princess are engaged. He should also be informed."

Jean-Paul, also standing, relaxed a bit. "I intend to stay here."

The queen studied him, then nodded, giving her permission for him to stay close to Megan. "I have duties," she murmured, annoyance showing through her anxiety for her daughter. "Selywyn will know how to reach me."

"I'll call you when we know something," Jean-Paul promised.

After the queen left, the doctor frowned his way. "You may use the sofa in here if you wish to sleep. However, there's no need for you to stay. Give the nurse your number and I'll call if there's a change."

"May I see Megan?"

"No."

This was said so quickly, so firmly, that his suspicions were at once awakened. Knowing he would get nothing more from the medical personnel, Jean-

Paul nodded and settled on the leather sofa, making his intentions plain.

Frowning, the doctor walked out and returned to the isolation wing. Jean-Paul stood and paced.

Megan was very ill. The doctor thought she might have something contagious, but he'd not been worried about the illness of the child from the children's hospital, so what could it be?

Perhaps the question he should have asked was, who was the person in room one and what did he or she have?

He had a feeling the royal physician wouldn't have been forthcoming with the information.

At midnight, he settled on the sofa with a blanket thoughtfully provided by a young nurse.

"This is unbelievable." Admiral Monteque glared at the royal physician.

The doctor shrugged and rubbed his eyes as if too weary to worry about what the admiral thought.

Selywyn studied the men in the king's council chamber with a sense of déjà vu. He and Logan were again in a meeting with the admiral, the doctor and Duke Pierceson Prescott. Again it concerned a strange malady affecting a member of the royal family.

"The queen has informed me there is a child," he now said to Dr. Waltham.

When the doctor hesitated, Monteque spoke out.

"It's in all the tabloids. Silvershire is reputedly the father."

Waltham nodded. "The earl is sleeping in my office as we speak. The queen says they are betrothed."

"Not officially," Selywyn said. "A contract must be worked out. The king has asked me to serve Penwyck in the matter. I will speak by telephone to Prince Bernier tomorrow. He takes a personal interest in the case, it seems, and holds his nephew in high esteem."

Monteque leaned forward. "Bernier has no male heir and his daughter is said to be flighty. Could he be thinking of his nephew as the next leader of Drogheda? That would be a new wrinkle."

"It's something to think about," Logan agreed. "But now we must worry about the entire royal family coming down with a disease for which the doctors have no explanation."

Waltham shook his head. "It's a mystery. Neither the king nor the princess evidenced signs of being bitten, so how could they get a viral disease in which the only known vector is a mosquito?"

"A needle?" Logan suggested. "AIDS can be spread by a needle used by an infected person."

"That's true," Waltham said, "but how could that happen in these two cases? One can hardly stick a royal without its being noticed." He glanced askance at the royal bodyguard, as if it might be his fault.

Logan gave him a grim stare. "The Black Knights could be in on it. Intelligence sources indicate they are opposed to the military alliance between Penwyck and Majorco. They would do anything to sabotage the agreement."

The Black Knights were a group of conspirators whose purpose was uncertain. Intelligence sources could gather little on them, except indications that such a group existed and they were intimately involved with Penwyck and all that happened on the island.

"It's too late for sabotage," Monteque said. "The agreement was ratified by the Privy Council. The public signing is scheduled for next month."

"But until then, the Majorcan king could possibly change his mind," Prescott said. "However, the alliance is to their advantage as much as ours."

"Let's reconsider," Selywyn said after a moment's silence. "Would anyone gain by either the king's or the princess's deaths?"

The men of the Royal Elite Team, including himself, could come up with no suggestions. Prince Owen, the probable heir, not only was out of the country, but all agreed he wasn't remotely a suspect. The royal children were honorable to the core.

"But there was one royal who was not," Monteque reminded them. "The king's twin."

Logan shook his head. "Prince Broderick has been in exile for twenty-five years. He has no private access to the royals. We watch him too closely.''

''Besides, a tropical fever is no guarantee of death,'' Waltham added. ''The king is far from dead. The princess is holding her own. So what is the point?''

''That is what we must determine,'' Prescott said. ''Is this some kind of red herring to distract us from the real issue?'' He frowned mightily. ''Again, what is the point? None that I can see.''

''Then we are stymied,'' the admiral said. He looked at the doctor. ''Keep us informed of any change.''

''I will have a proclamation issued so that all may hear and know,'' he said sarcastically and rose.

Selywyn walked the man to the door. ''Thank you for your input. I know you're doing all you can.''

Waltham smiled slightly. ''We've caught the princess in the early stages of the disease. As soon as we have confirmation, we'll start the treatment.''

''And the child?''

''That I can't tell you. It's in the hands of God.''

Selywyn returned to the others. ''Life is in the hands of God, but the perpetrator shall be in ours,'' he murmured.

''Amen,'' Logan echoed.

The meeting broke up shortly after midnight.

Chapter Twelve

Monday morning, Megan woke feeling irritable. The nurses surrounding her had refused to answer a single question. She ascertained for herself that her fever was down and the headache had receded to the back of her skull, where it was more manageable.

"I'm leaving," she declared after her restless night in the infirmary.

"Your Highness, you can't," the young nurse attending her morning ablutions objected.

"Huh. Watch me," Megan said with uncharacteristic belligerence.

The nurse hurried from the room. Dr. Waltham appeared in less than a minute.

"That was quick," Megan remarked.

"Where do you think you're going?" the doctor asked.

"To my quarters. I can be annoyed there just as well as here. I have things to do, such as the seminar you wanted."

"Forget the seminar. I'll handle it by phone." He gave her a severe frown although his kindly brown eyes twinkled. "Perhaps you need some company. There's a young man who spent the night on my office sofa and is demanding to see you."

"Jean-Paul?" she asked, sounding breathless and foolish beyond measure.

"One and the same," the doctor said wryly. "As for leaving, I'd like to keep you under observation for another day or two. For the baby's sake."

She laid a hand over her abdomen. "Is there danger to the child? I've read the flu virus can cause some harm."

"The placenta is usually a reliable barrier," he assured her. "You seem to be recovering without help, so I shouldn't worry about it."

Megan wondered if he was as confident as he sounded. But she had no reason to distrust the man who had helped bring her into the world. "Thank you, Dr. Waltham. I really am feeling much better. The headache is almost gone, just a dull throb now. My temperature was nearly normal this morning when the nurse took it."

He studied her as if curious about something, but

merely nodded his head. "Good. That's good. I'll send your young man in."

She flew out of bed when the doctor was gone and checked her hair and face in the bathroom mirror. She hadn't a smidgen of makeup, but maybe he would think she looked interestingly pale. She could practice being languid....

A giggle escaped her.

"You did that yesterday," a masculine voice said.

Jean-Paul strode into the room, looking like a young buccaneer in black jeans and a white shirt, the sleeves rolled up to reveal his muscular forearms. His smile was so bright and lovely it stole her breath right away.

I love him, she thought. *I really do love this man.* Her heart had known for ages, and she'd had a glimmer of it at the lodge—and perhaps on his yacht that magical night—but nothing like this.

The emotion wasn't anything as she'd dreamed it would be. She experienced the quiet certainty of it, as she would that of the sun rising or the weather changing or any one of a hundred day-to-day things she took for granted. And yet...and yet it was the wildest, most wondrous thing.

"How are you feeling?" he asked, stopping by her side. "Why are you out of bed?"

For a second, she couldn't answer. "I'm much better," she finally told him. She climbed into bed and modestly tightened the belt on her robe.

"Good. I was thinking about tearing the place apart if they didn't tell me something soon."

She stared at him. "Why?"

"I was worried." He grinned at her, looking younger and more daredevil than he ever had.

Megan clasped her hands and stared at them until her heart stopped bouncing off her rib cage. "That was kind."

A hand under her chin lifted her face to his. His eyes searched hers. "I'm not particularly kind," he said, almost as if he warned her not to expect it of him, "but I care for what is mine."

"What arrogance," she chided, but she couldn't help the smile that lingered on her lips.

"I know." He wasn't at all humble about it. "But I thought it best to let you know the facts straight away."

"I'm a modern woman. I will not be owned."

"Pledged, not owned," he conceded. "As I am pledged to you. The queen has declared us betrothed."

Megan was astounded. "She did? When?"

"Last night. To the doctor. The man is incredibly stubborn."

She had to bite her lip to keep from laughing at this observation from her betrothed.

Jean-Paul continued with his grievance. "He refused to let me stay with you during the night, but he says you are much improved this morning. The fever is gone.'' He laid a hand on her forehead and nodded as if satisfied.

His concern warmed her. The last feverish aches of the night vanished and she was comforted by his touch.

"Such magic,'' she whispered, taking his hand and holding it clasped between hers against her breast.

"Magic, yes, sweet selky.'' He kissed her lightly on the lips, his eyes growing darker as her breath caught with longing. "Ours will not be a cold marriage.''

"Have you known those that were?''

"We both have read of famous marriages that didn't last. Ours might be doubly difficult because of duty to our countries. What will your father expect?''

"I have no idea,'' she had to admit. "I've not spoken to him the past month for any length of time on private matters, other than the evening we told him of the child.''

"Nor have I.'' Jean-Paul frowned in concentration. "I saw your parents in the garden yesterday, though. Both appeared to be in good spirits. The king flirted with the queen.''

"Father?''

Jean-Paul nodded and gave her a sexy look. "He was quite romantic. He plucked a rose, kissed it, then held it to her lips. I think he might have kissed her, given a bit more time. Too bad Duke Logan chose that moment to interrupt with some message of national importance.''

Megan felt feverish again as she gazed into her lover's eyes and saw the hunger.

''Were I with my queen,'' he continued on a husky note, ''I would leave orders that no one should disturb us for less than a national crisis or else he might lose his head.''

The head nurse entered the room. ''Excuse me,'' she said without being the least interested in whether they did.

''Or she, as the case may be,'' Jean-Paul added under his breath.

Megan smothered a giggle as he flashed her a wicked grin and moved out of the way.

''More blood?'' Megan asked as the woman drew a vial of it. ''What, are we feeding a family of vampires?''

The nurse smiled at that. ''The doctor wants the lab to check this morning's results again. You seem to have a remarkable ability to recover.''

''From what?'' Jean-Paul asked.

''The virus,'' was all the closemouthed Dora would say.

''Do they know what kind of virus?'' Megan held a cotton swab over the wound when the nurse indicated she should. ''One of those twenty-four-hour things?''

''Something like that,'' Nurse Dora agreed and left.

"What a motormouth," Jean-Paul commented. "Hard to get her to stop yakking, isn't it?"

Megan laughed as he made a wry face. "I really feel much, much better. The doctor thinks the baby isn't harmed, especially since I threw the virus off so fast."

"A selky isn't very bothered by human things."

Sobering, she thought of the moments he'd referred to her as the mythical creature. "Is there a storm?"

"No. The sun is shining."

She nodded. "I wish we could go back..."

He took her hand and kissed the spot where she'd been punctured. "To the lodge? We will. I promise."

Believing him, she snuggled against the pillow and fell into a restful sleep. Each time she awoke during the day, Jean-Paul was there, either reading a magazine or napping in an easy chair. It was very comforting. She would tell Owen that she was happy with the betrothal. Tomorrow. For now, the headache was returning to the front of her skull, but merely as a low throb that didn't interfere with her dreams of a glorious future.

It was nearing midnight when Jean-Paul finally left Megan's side to go to his room and get some sleep. First he wanted to talk to Dr. Waltham.

Odd, the man never seemed to sleep but was at

the infirmary constantly. Was Megan's condition more serious than he had been led to believe?

The bossy head nurse had her back to him when he walked by her station and into the antechamber to the doctor's office. He stopped upon hearing a familiar voice.

"What are you saying?" the man demanded.

"Just what I said," the doctor replied, giving no ground to his irritable visitor.

"Then she couldn't have the virus."

Jean-Paul recognized the voice. Admiral Monteque, the elusive head of the Royal Navy, advisor to the king and Privy Council. He'd met with the man two more times in an effort to pin down the admiral's thoughts on Drogheda joining the military alliance of the islands.

"I assure you she does."

"But she's recovering?" Monteque's disbelief was palpable. "You must be mistaken."

"We've checked and rechecked. The princess appears to be overcoming the virus on her own. I see no need to start any other treatment, not at her present rate of recovery."

"Does this mean she is producing antibodies against the virus?" another man asked.

Sir Selywyn, the royal secretary, was with the other two men. Interesting.

"Yes, that would have to be the case," said the doctor.

Sir Selywyn spoke again. "Can you extract the antibodies from her blood?"

"First we would have to isolate and culture them. A person's blood carries antibodies to every microbe encountered during a lifetime. It isn't easy to find the right one."

Jean-Paul eavesdropped shamelessly on the trio as they discussed Megan's progress. He breathed a sigh of relief that she was on the road to health.

"The king—"

"Enough," snapped Monteque before the doctor could finish his thought.

"The king will be pleased at his daughter's progress," Sir Selywyn commented. He appeared at the doorway. "His lordship, the Earl of Silvershire," he murmured in an amused tone. "Join us. We were just discussing the princess's case. You know she is recovering?"

Jean-Paul entered the doctor's office. "Yes. I'm relieved. Have you told the queen?"

This little dig was aimed at the doctor, who had promised to keep them informed. The man looked a bit guilty but not at all repentant.

"I shall speak to her," Selywyn said. "I'm on my way for an audience now."

Jean-Paul made no comment, but he noted the man had access to the royal presence at…fifteen minutes before midnight, he saw by the clock on the doctor's desk. Why were so many astir in the palace at such an hour?

"Will you walk with me to the family quarters?" Selywyn asked him.

Jean-Paul nodded and went with the secretary after they bade the other two men good-night.

"You were good to stay with the princess," Selywyn told him as they climbed the stairs rather than taking the elevator from the underground infirmary. "The queen commented upon it. She was pleased."

"I was concerned for Megan. We are to be wed."

"So I understand. Congratulations. I have known Her Royal Highness since childhood and have watched her grow into a fine young woman."

"How long have you been secretary to the king?"

"Ten years, lacking three months."

Jean-Paul thought it was indicative of the man's nature to quote the precise time rather than rounding it off as most people would.

"How did you attain the position?"

Selywyn cast him an assessing perusal, then smiled dryly. "My father, before he retired, was a member of the Privy Council, elected by the township of Sterling. I had always intended to go into the king's service, either in the diplomatic corps or in the royal household. I became an aide on the king's staff. When the old secretary retired, he recommended me to the king."

"You serve very well, from all reports," Jean-

Paul said and meant it. The man was known for his loyalty to the royal family and to Penwyck.

Selywyn merely inclined his head. "I'm glad you and the princess have decided on the marriage."

"You approve?"

"Indeed. She has chosen you, and I have never doubted her judgment."

Jean-Paul smiled. "It's good to have a friend close to the king. I fear he considers the union questionable."

They arrived outside the queen's private quarters. "Take care that the princess knows your heart," the secretary advised. "It would ease her mind over the future, I think. She is the Quiet One, but her feelings are no less deep for not expressing them as openly as others."

"I know." Jean-Paul bade the man good-night and went to his own rooms. It was a long time before he fell asleep as he mulled over all the nuances in the conversations he'd heard that day. His last thought was of Megan and the relief he'd felt upon knowing she was getting well.

That put him in a much better frame of mind, and so he slept, his dreams of open seas filled with mythical creatures such as mermaids and sad-eyed selkies who wouldn't hold still for his touch...

Jean-Paul was awakened early on Tuesday morning by the shrill ringing of the coded cell phone.

"What is going on?" his uncle, Prince Bernier of Drogheda, demanded.

"Good morning, Uncle," Jean-Paul said, sitting up and glancing at the clock. Seven-thirty. He hit the alarm before it could go off just as a soft knock sounded on the door. "Come in," he called.

A footman entered, bringing a tray with coffee and the breakfast as he'd requested the previous night. He dismissed the servant.

"I'm sorry. What was your question?" he asked the prince.

"The papers are full of the great romance between you and Megan of Penwyck. Your father confirms that marriage is in the works. A Sir Selwyn contacted our foreign minister about the contract yesterday. Why am I the last to know?"

Jean-Paul poured a cup of coffee while he apologized. He took a sip and gazed at the cover over his breakfast plate. He was famished this morning. "The tabloids deal in speculation. We've only recently decided on marriage."

"Why was I not informed the minute it became a possibility?" the prince demanded imperiously. "We must consider the implications and decide what we shall demand in the marriage contract."

Jean-Paul suppressed a spurt of anger. "Megan and I have some problems to work out."

"Is it true she expects a child?"

"Yes."

"Yours?"

"Yes." Jean-Paul couldn't prevent the warning note in the word. He would not have Megan disparaged.

His uncle hesitated, then laughed. "You aren't usually so hotheaded. It must be love."

At the silence that followed, Jean-Paul knew the prince expected a reply. "Naturally there are feelings. Neither the princess nor I want a state marriage. This is private—"

"Nonsense," the prince interrupted. "This is perfect, just perfect. Hmm, this is the last Tuesday of the month, too late to try for a June wedding. I don't suppose we could have the wedding in Drogheda?"

"I hardly think so."

"No, Penwyck wouldn't stand for that," his uncle agreed, obviously not noticing the frost in his nephew's tone. The prince chuckled. "But they can't refuse the alliance after the marriage, either. Good thinking there."

"I'm afraid I can't take credit," Jean-Paul said dryly. "The thought didn't enter my mind. Nor yours. You didn't ask me to be your emissary until after the ambassador fell ill."

"All worked out for the best. Fate is on our side in this," the prince declared with all the lofty assurance of a monarch used to being obeyed.

Jean-Paul glanced upward, seeking patience, and said nothing.

"I will make her a magnificent gift. What do you think of the heirloom emeralds?"

Jean-Paul was startled. "Those are usually reserved for the bride of the reigning prince."

"I have no son," the prince reminded him. "I can hardly give them to my daughter's husband. As a wedding gift to both of you, I am thinking of the Warwyck estate. A Penwyck ancestor built it when he thought he had Drogheda conquered. He never got to live in it." Prince Bernier chuckled in gleeful satisfaction.

"That would be more than generous, Uncle. I promise to call you the moment we have a firm date."

"What should we expect as a dowry?"

Resentment flared in Jean-Paul. "I don't expect anything, but I'm sure the ministers from each country will work it out to the satisfaction of everyone involved."

The prince gave him several instructions on the wedding and the agreement, which he only half listened to. When they hung up, Jean-Paul ate his breakfast while his thoughts churned within him.

The rebel in him wanted to thumb his nose at protocol. No wonder Megan didn't want to marry. It wasn't the union of a male and female, but of two countries, each seeking an advantage over the other through the bridal contract. For a moment, he actually contemplated sailing away with Megan and

marrying in some foreign land where no one knew
them.

As if they could.

He considered how his life had changed in two
short weeks. It had been two weeks ago yesterday
that he'd gotten Megan's request for a meeting.
He'd immediately put aside everything to come to
her. Two weeks. Now he was nearly a married man.
In less than seven months he would be a father.

Smiling at the twists of fate, he finished the meal,
showered, then went to see his bride. The nurse
barred his way. "The princess isn't feeling well,"
she told him.

"What has happened?"

The woman hesitated, then said, "The fever is
up again. The doctor is with her."

Jean-Paul deftly stepped around the nurse. "I'll
speak with him."

Ignoring her angry huff, he went into the isolation wing of the infirmary. Megan was alone and
sleeping soundly. Jean-Paul looked up and down
the hallway.

The doctor came out of the room opposite hers.
He started upon seeing Jean-Paul, then came forward with a weary smile. He pressed a finger over
his lips and pulled Megan's door closed. "I don't
want her disturbed."

"She's worse?"

"A relapse. These things happen."

Jean-Paul gestured across the hall. "Who is in the other room?"

"No one," the doctor said quickly.

"I think you lie." Jean-Paul started toward the door.

The doctor caught his arm. "It is no one important. A minor clerk in the foreign office who took sick after returning home to visit his parents."

"He has the same illness as Megan?"

Dr. Waltham nodded, his gaze on Megan's door. "Her fever is my fault. I asked that she arrange a seminar. When she came down here to check the arrangements with me, she must have contracted the virus..."

When he trailed off, Jean-Paul demanded, "How?"

"That is what has us baffled. The carrier is usually a mosquito, although it's possible to transmit encephalitis through a fly or other biting bug."

Jean-Paul stiffened with shock. "She has viral encephalitis? Isn't that usually fatal?"

"Not if it's put into remission before somnolence occurs. We have medicines. I hesitate to use them because of the child."

A chill settled along Jean-Paul's spine like the cold hand of death.

"She's strong, more than we ever imagined," Waltham said in assuring tones. "She's holding her own."

"But?" Jean-Paul demanded, sensing there was more.

"The child might not be so lucky. At this early stage of development, if the placenta is breached, the virus can harm the fetus."

"In what manner?"

Waltham sighed grimly. "Brain damage. Malformations of body systems. Deformity."

"God," Jean-Paul muttered, and rubbed a hand over his face as despair such as he'd never known raged through him.

"You must be prepared," Waltham continued. "Megan doesn't know yet. You must help her through this. Perhaps it would be better—"

Jean-Paul waited, but the doctor said nothing more, only looked at him with sadness in his eyes. "An abortion?" Jean-Paul asked.

Waltham nodded. "First we can check the fetus by sonogram and perhaps tell if there's any harm."

Undefined feelings congealed into a painful mass in Jean-Paul's chest. "I want to stay with her...to be with her when she wakes."

The doctor nodded, looking too tired to argue.

Jean-Paul slipped quietly into her room and stood looking at her flushed face. She was so still, lying there as if life had already left her.

All the moments they'd spent together flashed through his mind. Megan at seventeen, her face glowing, their walk along the cove, the depths he'd sensed in her even then. Her picture in the paper at twenty-two, a university senior in Art and History, with a minor in the Humanities, graduating with honors.

Megan at twenty-seven, delivering a speech before an international body of diplomats and world-class businessmen, competent and intelligent.

And finally that last night of the trade conference, when she had come to him...

Those moments, the delight and wonder of her, mingled with the present and his fears for her and the child they had made that night. Realization gathered in him, a heavy ball of self-knowledge that ripped pride and arrogance to shreds and left his heart open and raw.

This woman. This one slight female. She was his fate, his future, his one true love...

He clasped her hand. "You'll not leave me like this, selky," he ordered, his voice hoarse and urgent. "I mean it. You won't. Do you hear me?"

Green eyes opened slightly. "Yes," she whispered, but her voice was weak.

"You will not leave me," he whispered fiercely. "You are my heart, my desire, my life's mate. You are all that's good within me. I love you...you, only you."

She stared at him a second longer, then her lashes fluttered closed.

Darkness spiraled into his soul as she slipped further and further from him, edging toward the coma that could claim her life. The lonely call of his heart went without answer.

Chapter Thirteen

Megan awoke to a startled cry, then realized she was the one who made the sound. Glancing rapidly around the room, she saw she was still in the infirmary. A head rested on the mattress by her side. She ran her hand into Jean-Paul's dark hair, liking the warmth of his scalp under her fingers as she wondered if it was night or day.

Jean-Paul sat up and rubbed his eyes, then gazed at her. Dark beard accentuated the line of his jaw and throat.

"What day is it?" she asked, sounding oddly croaky.

"Thursday."

"What happened to Wednesday?"

"You slept through it, also most of Tuesday."

"Is it morning or night?"

"Morning. Around six. They'll bring breakfast soon." He touched her forehead. "You're cool again."

She frowned, trying to recall something. "I was cold during the night."

"Chills. That was yesterday afternoon and early in the evening." He poured a glass of water and held the straw to her lips so she could drink. She did so thirstily.

"You've grown a beard. Were you here all night?"

"Yes."

"Why?" Her voice was hardly above a whisper.

He finished off the rest of the water before meeting her eyes. "You know, selky," he told her softly.

"I dreamed...I think I dreamed that you said... was it true? Or were you saying it to make me feel better."

She saw his chest lift in a deep breath. He exhaled like one admitting defeat. "I said it because it's true." He leaned close and pressed his face into her hair. "I love you, Megan of Penwyck."

She smiled. "So it wasn't a dream."

"No." He lifted his head and glared at her. "You damn well better love me back. I'm not going through this misery alone."

Laughter bubbled in her, overflowed and filled the room with her surprise and joy.

He managed to hold on to his glare another minute, then he grinned. "Say it," he said, and gave her shoulders a little shake.

But she was suddenly shy. She tugged his head down so she could whisper, "I do. I love you. Very much."

His chuckle was wry. "How soon can we be married? I find myself an exceedingly eager bridegroom."

"Within a month?"

"Yes. I will speed things along." Then he whispered other things to her that were lovely to hear, and she whispered back with all the longing of her heart. They were still planning the future when their breakfasts arrived: sausage and an omelette and toast for him, porridge and red fruit-flavored gelatin for her.

"Huh," she groused. "Why do I get this while you get all the good stuff?"

"Charm," he said loftily. "Nurse Dora is mad about me."

They were still laughing when the queen came in.

Queen Marissa paused on the threshold of the room and listened to her daughter's and Jean-Paul's soft laughter.

So much happiness. Tears burned behind her

eyes. It was every mother's wish for her children. For Megan, her quiet child, she wanted a world of love and joy. Looking at the faces of the young lovers, she knew they had found all their hearts' desires.

"Mother, please come in," Megan called out, spotting her standing there observing them.

Marissa went to the bed and kissed Megan's forehead. "The doctor tells me you are on the mend. Again."

"I think it's real this time. I feel wonderful. No headache. No muscle pains."

"And you, Jean-Paul?" the queen inquired. "Nurse Dora tells me you haven't left this room in two days."

"I was worried about Megan."

The earl looked charmingly disheveled with a dark beard on his cheeks. His hair was tousled and showed a tendency to wave naturally. His white shirt had definitely been slept in. Its wrinkles looked permanently creased.

A handsome pirate, she thought, this rogue who had stolen her daughter's heart.

Her own heart contracted in hope and longing. She had thought the king might come to her last night, but after many restless hours she realized that wasn't to be. She'd considered going to him, but some small doubt had made her hesitate, then decide against it.

It was odd to no longer know the man she'd been married to for thirty years.

"Are we planning a royal wedding?" she asked.

The couple locked hands and nodded together.

Again the queen felt the hot sting of tears at the young people's mutual feelings. Really, she had to stop this or she would be a blubbering idiot at the wedding.

"As soon as possible, please," Jean-Paul requested.

"Yes. I promise to rush things along," she told them. She briefly laid a hand on Megan's tummy where her first grandchild was developing. "The little one is fine?"

She saw a muscle jerk in Jean-Paul's jaw. Fear intruded on the happy atmosphere.

"I think so," Megan said, but she was watching her fiancé in a slightly puzzled manner. "The doctor didn't say…" She stopped as worry entered her eyes. "Did he say anything to you?" she asked Jean-Paul.

He leaned his elbows on the bed and pressed her hand to his lips before replying. "There's no way to tell if there's harm—"

"Like what?" Megan interrupted. "What kind of harm?"

"It was a virus, love," he murmured soothingly. "There could be complications. However, the chances of injury to the child are probably slight since your body threw off the infection so readily."

"But if it reached the baby—"

The queen's heart ached as her daughter abruptly stopped speaking and absorbed all the implications.

"Then we'll face that when we know for sure. There are tests we can have done, sonograms and such."

Megan laid a hand over her abdomen. She suddenly smiled. "It's okay. I know the child is okay."

Jean-Paul touched her forehead in a loving manner. "I think so, too. But if it isn't, there will be other babies, my lovely selky, I promise you that."

Their love was so sweet, so fresh and new, filled with all the hope of youth and ideals. The queen pressed a hand to her throat and withdrew from the room. Some moments weren't meant to be shared.

"Your Majesty," Dr. Waltham said, coming across the broad corridor and bowing over her hand. "The princess is doing quite well. The lab could find no traces of the virus in her blood this morning. A miracle, it is."

"The miracle of love, I think, Doctor. Megan has much to live for."

Waltham gazed into her eyes. "She does indeed. She is as beautiful in spirit as in the flesh. As with her mother, the gods smile kindly upon her. You are feeling well?"

The queen, meeting the doctor's eyes, realized with a jolt that the man was looking at her with grave tenderness. Then his expression became that of the royal physician once more. She might have imagined the emotion.

"Yes, I'm fine, thank you. So are Meredith and Anastasia. I have been keeping an eye on them. They don't seem in the least affected by this mysterious virus. How could Megan have gotten such a thing? There have been no reports of illness in the kingdom."

"Perhaps a chance contact while she was at the international trade conference two months ago," Waltham suggested. "We are checking out the possibility, discreetly, of course."

"Two months? Is that the incubation period?"

"It can be two days, two months or longer. Viral strains are unpredictable at best. We are trying to isolate and identify it."

The doctor looked somewhat chagrined, as if he'd disclosed more than he'd meant. The queen sensed nuances she didn't understand. "Is there a chance of an epidemic?" she asked quietly, already preparing, in her mind, the steps to see them through a national emergency.

"No, no, nothing like that," the doctor assured her. "I'm sure this is an isolated incident. One of those things that happen with no rhyme or reason." He smiled encouragingly, then looked relieved when a nurse approached and told him he had a call.

Queen Marissa glanced around the quiet infirmary and started toward the door across from Megan's room without quite thinking about why she suddenly felt a need to investigate.

"Please, Your Majesty," the head nurse called out, coming down the hall with her quick, silent tread. "This room is under quarantine."

"Who is in there?"

"No one. The patient has gone home, but the room has been sprayed with a disinfectant solution that mustn't be disturbed for several days."

"Did the patient have the same thing as my daughter?"

Nurse Dora hesitated. "I don't know. He had a fever and muscular aches, the same as the princess."

"But he recovered, too?"

"Yes."

The queen narrowed her eyes on the nurse, but the woman didn't glance away. Satisfied that was the truth, Queen Marissa nodded and returned to her quarters. She had a full schedule to get through that day. She would have Gwen, her lady-in-waiting and confidante, check on Megan's progress and keep her informed by the hour.

Please, no more relapses, she prayed as she took the elevator to the upper level.

"Yes. Yes. Deliriously happy," Megan said to her brother, Owen. "The wedding is next month. You'd better be home for it," she warned with a dire threat in her tone.

She hung up the phone beside her bed. It was good to be in her own familiar room in the palace. Glancing up, she met the smiling look Jean-Paul bestowed on her.

"Both your brothers have reported in," he said. "Will you stop worrying about them now?"

Ignoring his mock-serious frown, she nodded. "They are adventurers at heart. I wonder if either will be satisfied being tied to official duties as king."

A flicker of emotion showed in his beautiful blue eyes, then was gone.

"What?" she asked. "Is something worrying you?"

He shook his head. "My uncle wishes to give us an estate in Drogheda for a wedding present. I fear we must live there at least part of the time." He smiled in resignation. "It is a lovely place that borders the sea. You'll like that."

"It sounds wonderful." She thought any place where her lover was would be heaven, but she refrained from voicing the sentiment. That he had her whole heart he already knew.

"Wherever we are together will be paradise," he murmured. "There is another problem."

Her heart contracted slightly, but nothing could destroy the peace she felt inside. "Tell me."

"The prince is sending out hints that he is considering a royal heir to the principality."

"He has a daughter."

"It must be a male, according to law."

"The daughter has a husband. Doesn't he have royal connections to Majorco?"

"Yes, but…"

She was silent as the full impact hit her. "Prince Bernier is thinking of you?"

"He hasn't said outright, but there is that possibility." He sighed, then laughed softly.

Megan frowned, thinking of all the official duties they would have to perform if that was the case. "Our lives will have to be very circumspect," she finally said.

"Not all the time. There will be moments when we shall be alone…when I will summon my selky to come join me in the sea. There we will play to our heart's content."

Leaning forward, his elbows propped on the bed, he sealed the words with a kiss.

The kiss started out as very tender, then rapidly escalated into hunger.

"Stay with me tonight," she whispered.

"I don't think I could hold you in a chaste embrace," he admitted, "and you aren't well enough for passion."

"We shall see about that." She wrapped her arms around his neck and gave a mighty tug.

Jean-Paul let himself be pulled into the bed. Carefully keeping his weight off her, he let them engage in playful passion for long, sweet moments.

Just as things were getting particularly interesting, a shriek rent the air.

"I'm so sorry, Your Royal Highness," Candy said, red faced. "I'll return later. Just send for me. If you need me, that is. That is…if…when…" The maid fled the room.

He gave his future bride a rueful smile. "A forecast of things to come, I fear."

"It doesn't matter," Megan assured him. "Let's just remember to reserve private moments for our family, just us and our children. Then we can bear anything else."

Gazing into her earnest face, he realized anew that this was the woman of his heart. There was the rebellious part of her that she kept under control, just as he did, but there would be moments that were theirs.

Like the night on the ship.

Like the moments at the mountain lodge.

Like this one.

"Selky," he said just before he kissed her again. "Together we are the magic."

Her eyes glowed when she looked at him. "Together," she said, and showered him with enchantment through her touch.

His restless spirit stilled as love filled his soul. It was more than he'd ever imagined, more than enough for a lifetime.

Megan basked in the warmth that flooded her like a great tide. Love was a vast ocean, she thought as she snuggled into her lover's embrace. The ebb and flow of life moved through them. She sensed the child, secure within her, and knew it would be a fine baby, loved and protected by its parents and grandparents and all in their combined families.

A link to the future.

No matter what it might bring, whether increased duties and a more public life than either of them wanted, she would make sure there were many private moments, too. She had the example of her own parents to go by. So did Jean-Paul.

She'd spoken to his parents, and they were very supportive of the couple. That was nice.

From the island in the cove, she heard the bark of a seal. From far out at sea, another answered, its call lonely and distressed.

Smiling, Megan knew the one on the island called the other to land. "Home, selky," she murmured to the wandering one. It was the best place to be.

*   *   *   *   *

magazine

♥ ───────────────────────────── **quizzes**

Is he the one? What kind of lover are you? Visit the **Quizzes** area to find out!

♥ ─────────────────── **recipes for romance**

Get scrumptious meal ideas with our **Recipes for Romance**.

♥ ─────────────────────── **romantic movies**

Peek at the **Romantic Movies** area to find Top 10 Flicks about First Love, ten Supersexy Movies, and more.

♥ ───────────────────────── **royal romance**

Get the latest scoop on your favorite royals in **Royal Romance**.

♥ ─────────────────────────────── **games**

Check out the **Games** pages to find a ton of interactive romantic fun!

♥ ─────────────────────── **romantic travel**

In need of a romantic rendezvous? Visit the **Romantic Travel** section for articles and guides.

♥ ───────────────────────────── **lovescopes**

Are you two compatible? Click your way to the **Lovescopes** area to find out now!

where love comes alive—online...

SINTMAG

When California's most talked about dynasty is threatened, only family, privilege and the power of love can protect them!

THE COLTONS

Coming in May 2002

THE HOPECHEST BRIDE

by
Kasey Michaels

Cowboy Josh Atkins is furious at Emily Blair, the woman he thinks is responsible for his brother's death...so *why* is he so darned attracted to her? After dark accusations—and sizzling sparks—start to fly between Emily and Josh, they both realize that they can make peace...and love!

Available at your favorite retail outlet.

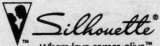

Award-winning author
SHARON DE VITA
brings her special brand of romance to

Silhouette

SPECIAL EDITION™

and

SILHOUETTE *Romance*™

in her new cross-line miniseries

SADDLE FALLS

This small Western town was rocked by scandal when the youngest son of the prominent Ryan family was kidnapped. Watch as clues about the mysterious disappearance are unveiled—and meet the sexy Ryan brothers...along with the women destined to lasso their hearts.

Don't miss:

WITH FAMILY IN MIND
February 2002, Silhouette Special Edition #1450

ANYTHING FOR HER FAMILY
March 2002, Silhouette Romance #1580

A FAMILY TO BE
April 2002, Silhouette Romance #1586

A FAMILY TO COME HOME TO
May 2002, Silhouette Special Edition #1468

Available at your favorite retail outlet.

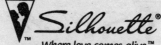

Silhouette®

Where love comes alive™